SALTY BRINE BEACH

THE LIGHTHOUSE SERIES
BOOK 2

JUDY PRESCOTT MARSHALL

JUDY PRESCOTT MARSHALL

For more information please address ~

Writing Studio 12 May Knoll Dover Plains, NY 12522

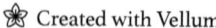 Created with Vellum

For My Husband

1

———

David sat quietly on his back deck watching ships and sail boats glide past the house. To his right, the ferry was leaving the harbor for open waters. The water seemed calm with a hint of gentle surf tides. Next to the lifeguard tower three men and one woman dressed in a red one-piece bathing suit were talking. One of the men pointed toward the public restrooms and coin-operated hot showers. David raised his eyes to see if she headed his way or back in the water. A second later, his cellphone rang. He smiled seeing the caller was Shelby, another bathing beauty. "Hello," he said with a smile on his face.

"It's not too early, is it?"

David laughed aloud. "No, you know me. Up before the sun makes an appearance or my day is ruined."

She laughed before saying, "Great, so you jogged, had your coffee and you're ready for the day."

"You could say that" he replied and went into the kitchen to put his cup in the dishwasher. "What's up with you?"

"I have the remaining pictures for the inn."

David smiled with excitement. He loved every photo she took for the rooms, dining rooms, lobby and in the banquet room. "Wow, that was fast. Do you want to meet this week or—"

"Today, works for me. Are you free around ten?"

David looked up at the calendar and said, "Yes, that sounds good. Do you want to meet me at the inn?"

"Actually, I have a surprise for you. Can I stop by your house, and we can go to the inn together?"

"Of course, I'll cut your check as well."

Shelby told David the balance due and said she would be there in two hours. After she hung up the phone, she picked up the photo of Aunt Emily and smiled hoping David was going to love it as much as she did.

David set his cellphone on the charger, turned the music on in the living room and cranked up the sound. KOOL 1180 Oldies was playing, "Sea of Love". David sang along as he jumped in the shower. At a quarter to ten, he turned the volume down on the stereo and poured two glasses of iced tea. He added a fresh mint leaf to Shelby's and a slice of lemon to his own. He set two slices of Aunt Emily's chocolate chip pound cake on a small plate and carried the tray to the living area. When he heard the knock on the front door he turned the stereo off.

David opened the door and put his hand on his heart when he saw the photo of Aunt Emily standing on the beach with the sun setting behind her. Her gray hair radiant, her hazel eyes sparkled in the light and her cheeks were flush from the excitement of her newest cookbook hitting the bestseller's list before it even went on sale. "Oh, Shelby," David said as he reached out to take the photo from her. "This is great." He leaned in for a hug. "You know how to capture a moment."

Shelby smiled with confidence knowing he was happy. "I'm so glad you like it. I saw her standing there and had to get a snapshot."

"Come on in, I poured us a glass of iced tea and I have Aunt Emily's pound cake. Let's sit in the living room." David set the photo of Aunt Emily on the mantle above the fireplace. Picked up Shelby's check and handed it to her. "I can't thank you enough for all the gorgeous pictures. The guests comment on every picture."

"David, this is very generous of you. Way more than I quoted."

He held his hand out for her to take a seat. "Please, you saved me from shopping, and you made my life easier. I can't thank you enough for putting your heart into every photo. The one in the lobby is breathtaking. I find myself standing in front of it for long periods of time. The way you captured the sun going down behind the inn... outstanding."

"Thank you," she replied and said, "Taking photos during the golden hour is my favorite time of day."

A half-hour later, David and Shelby climbed into her Jeep and headed for the inn. They were standing in the gym, hanging the photos of a surfer, a kayaker and one of a couple hang gliding when David's manager handed him the cordless phone. David held the hammer out to Shelby and said, "Give me one second." Then he stepped to the side. "Hello."

"David, it's Grace. I have been calling you all morning. I'm at South County Hospital with Aunt Emily."

David almost dropped the phone, his face was serious, his eyes moist. His voice was low. "Is she... okay?"

"I received a call from Maria. Apparently, she slipped on

wet grass while gardening. She's in good spirits but needs surgery."

"Surgery?" David said and looked at Shelby in despair.

Shelby put the hammer down, held the palm of her hands up and whispered, "Is everything okay?" Then she moved closer to where David was standing.

"I'm on my way," David said and handed the phone back to his manager. "Aunt Emily is at South County—"

"Let's go," Shelby announced, and they bolted for the door. "What happened?"

"Grace said she slipped and needs surgery."

"Oh, geez. I hope she didn't break her hip," Shelby said as she climbed into her Jeep. "I know a shortcut. Don't worry, she'll be fine. She's tough."

David sat stoic for what seemed a long time. "I don't know what I would do if something happened to her."

Seven minutes later, Shelby pulled up to the emergency department and told David to go inside while she parked the car. "I'll find you."

David tapped her on the hand. "Thank you." As soon as he entered the double glass entryway, he was met by Grace.

Grace was rubbing her hands nervously together as she explained. "She said she was wearing the wrong footwear. Apparently, she had her smooth bottom Muck boots on and slipped while pulling a garden wagon behind her."

Shelby entered, stood next to David giving his elbow a quick squeeze. Grace can feel a smile curve involuntarily as she asked. "Were the two of you together?"

David offered an unimpressed furrow with his left brow. "Shelby and I were hanging pictures at the inn when you called. Where's Aunt Emily?"

"I'll wait here," Shelby said as David followed Grace down the corridor.

David hugged Aunt Emily so tight she had to push him back. "I broke my foot, let's keep my ribs in tack." She laughed. "Stop worrying. You know I hate when you get that look on your face."

David grabbed her hand and said, "I love you more than life and you know it. What happened?"

"I was pulling the garden wagon down to the perennial garden and I must have slipped, before I knew it the wagon was pushing me faster and faster down the hill." She rolled her eyes. "That's when the damn thing knocked me over."

An hour later, they came into the room and took Aunt Emily upstairs for surgery. The nurse assured David it was an easy repair. By three o'clock that afternoon, Aunt Emily was back in her room. Every hour on the hour, the doctor came in and asked her what her pain level was, each time Aunt Emily assured her she was not in any pain and wanted to go home. At seven o'clock that evening, Aunt Emily told the doctor she gave her foot to God and was ready to leave.

David smiled at the doctor and said, "I guess she's ready to go home."

2

———

Ella wanted to say no, but how could she? The woman was one of her best customers. She literally spent enough money at Ella's boutique to cover the electric and the heating bills. "I'm so sorry to hear about your friend. Yes, I would be honored to take her place," she told the bride. Ella hung up the phone and wanted to scream. Going to a wedding where she wouldn't know a single soul was not on her list of priorities, especially considering her new spring line was due to arrive any day. With Ava in Point Judith, Ella had her hands full... literally. Working ten-hours a day, six days a week and on Monday—her only day off, she still found herself going over the books, ensuring all the orders were delivered and to the proper location. God forbid; Ava received two boxes of sun hats... again. The phone rang. This time she glanced at the caller ID before picking it up and saying, "The Beach Boutique, Ella speaking."

"Ella, I have a delivery from Bali Swimwear that requires a signature. I'm at your Point Judith location and there's a sign on the door. What do you want me to do with the order?"

Ella looked up at the clock. It was almost eleven. "Hang on, let me call Ava."

"Yeah, I tried that; it goes right to her voicemail."

Ella took in a deep frustrating breath before asking, "By any chance do you have another delivery in the area? Perhaps I could call a friend of mine to meet you back there and sign for the package."

"I do as a matter of fact. It's on Pier Market Place. I wouldn't have called you except there's a label on here that says, RUSH ORDER."

"I appreciate you calling me. Let me call Grace and have her meet you there in fifteen minutes."

Ella hung up the phone and immediately called Grace. "Grace, thank God you answered the phone. Ava is MIA again. I have a delivery that requires a signature. Can you please run over to the store and sign for it?"

"Wait! What? What do you mean Ava is missing... again." Grace reached down and grabbed her pocketbook. "Of course, I'll head over there right now."

Ella inhaled a sigh of relief. "Apparently, there is a sign on the door."

"What the hell does it say?" Grace asked as she got in her car.

"The deliver guy didn't read it to me, he just said no one was at the store."

"Take a deep breath, I'll find her. Good Lord what is she up to now? Did you try her cell?"

"Yes, and it goes right to voicemail which mean she has her cellphone turned off. When you located her ass, please have her call me. Hey, thanks for doing this. I believe she took orders for some of the swimwear in the package, so she needs this box."

"Gotcha. Okay, I'm here. No delivery truck. Where is everyone else? Why are the lights off?"

Ella could hear Grace calling out for Ava. "Ava. Yeah, no one is here."

"The full-time staff don't start until the end of May. We were trying to save money. Ava said she could handle opening and closing."

"I'll stay here until she comes. If I have any questions, I'll call you." Grace looked out the window as the truck pulled up to the front door. "Your delivery is here. Don't worry, I've got your back." Grace disconnected the call and signed for the boxes. "Thank you for coming back," she said and waved goodbye.

Grace hung the OPEN flag, turned on all the lights and began to unbox the swimwear. "Gorgeous," she said as she reached for a rust colored-one-piece, stood in front of the mirror and held it under her chin. Then she set it on the table with the others. An hour later, she had her first customer come through the door. "Hi, I'm Grace. If you need any help... I'll try my best to assist you."

The woman smiled before saying, "Don't get too close to me." She sniffled. "I have a cold. I'm looking for a gift to send to my best friend for her birthday."

"Don't worry about it. My four-year-old has a runny nose all the time. Do you have an idea what you're looking for or price range, maybe I can guide you in the right direction."

The woman looked up at the nautical sweater hanging above the racks and pointed. "She would love that sweater."

"Great, what size?"

"Small, she's a size four when she's soaking wet." The

woman laughed. "She's vegan. Only eats healthy food. Unlike me, I devour everything put in front of me."

Grace waved her hand at the woman. "You have a fabulous figure."

"Bless your heart," the woman replied. "You know what, give me one too. A size large, please."

As soon as Grace rang-up that customer, three more came in, and by the time she was ready to close, she had taken care of a dozen or so customers, including a few men. Several times throughout the day, Ella texted her to make sure she was okay and to see if Ava made it to the store. At four o'clock she called Ella to let her know she was closing the store so she could go and pick up Hudson from day care.

Ella picked up on the first ring. "Any sign of Ava?"

Grace shook her head. "No, I texted her, I called her phone so much her mailbox is full."

"Yeah, I have been calling her all day too. Were you busy today?"

"I sold a little over twenty-one-hundred-dollars," Grace said as she shut the lights. "Listen, I would stay until closing, but I need to pick Hudson up. If you want, we can come back."

"No, please, you did enough. Thank you."

Grace turned the sign to close, brought the flag inside and locked the door. "Hey, I forgot to tell you, Aunt Emily fell the other day."

"Oh no," Ella replied. "What happened? Is she okay?"

"She'll be fine. She broke her ankle gardening. Apparently, she slipped on the wet grass while pulling the garden cart behind her. It literally pushed her down the hill before it knocked her over."

"I'll bet you have your hands full now." Ella said as she closed her eyes in a long blink.

"Actually, Shelby is staying at the house with her. I think her and David are seeing each other. She was with him at the hospital," Grace said, but immediately regretted her words.

Silence. Grace held her breath.

Ella stopped herself from saying how she really felt about David and Shelby. The day she left Point Judith to go back to Connecticut, was hard enough. She closed her eyes remembering the last thing David said to her. "Please choose Point Judith, it's the most beautiful place on earth." If only you and Grace didn't share so many lasting memories.

"I'm sorry. I shouldn't have told you that," Grace said knowing Ella had feelings for David.

"It's fine. I chose to live and work in Connecticut. I had my chance, right?"

"I love you, Ella."

"I love you more, Grace. Give Aunt Emily a hug from me. Kiss Hudson and go find our girl."

The call ended as Ella's heart thrashed against her ribs.

3

Grace picked Hudson up just in time to see him receive his first kiss from the cutest little girl. Bethany had long brown hair, big brown eyes and a dimple on her right cheek when she smiled.

The sun was high in the sky, the temperature outside was perfect. Grace felt a rush of excitement come over her watching her son. She missed his father, but in her heart, she knew he was with her in the delivery room and right by her side watching their son blush with exhilaration. She waved to the other mother and held her hands out to Hudson for a hug.

Hudson ran to her, wiped his cheek and said, "Yuck!"

Grace smiled at him and said, "Stop. It was a very nice gesture. Maybe, she likes you."

Hudson gave his mother a smirk before saying, "She made me a friendship bracelet. I'm not wearing it." Then he handed it to Grace.

Grace put it on her own wrist and said, "I think today calls for ice cream at The Sweet Spot."

That put a smile on Hudson's face. Hand in hand, they

walked to the ice cream parlor. "How about we stop by and see Aunt Emily afterwards?"

"Will Uncle David be there?"

"I don't know. Maybe?" Several times, Grace caught Hudson looking at the bracelet, each time he glanced at it, he smiled a little more.

On the drive over to Aunt Emily's, Grace thought about Hudson growing up without any siblings. She wanted him to have a little brother and a sister. She started breathing heavier, her heart was rising and falling as she pondered the thought of asking David if he would donate his sperm. "Huh," she said aloud.

"Mommy, did you say something?"

Grace gave Hudson a pointed look of wordless motion in the rear-view mirror before saying, "No, baby, sorry Mommy was thinking out loud." She put her elbow on the door, rested her head on the palm of her hand and continued driving, wondering, and dreaming about more children. As soon as she parked the car, her phone chimed. "Hang-on baby. I need to answer this."

"Who is it, Mommy?"

"Aunt Ella." Grace texted her back. "What? Hell no!" Then she dialed her number. "What the hell did you sign up for?"

"Mommy, you said a bad word."

"Sorry, baby. I won't say it again. Why did you agree to do it?"

Ella explained. "I agreed to be a bridesmaid, I never would have expected her maid of honor to ask me to chip in on the shower gift or to partake in all the activities."

"Just tell her no. That's absurd."

"Tell me about it. As it is, I agreed to buy the dress. Hey, any word from Ava?"

"No, I'll drop by her house as soon as I check on Aunt Emily."

"Oh, okay. Give everyone a hug from me. Talk to you later." Ella disconnected the call.

Grace looked at her cell, wishing Ella had moved to Point Judith.

"Okay, let's go see how Aunt Emily is doing today."

She unbuckled him, held his hand and rang the doorbell. A slender woman wearing a black dress and white apron opened the door.

"Welcome, may I ask your name," she said and smiled warmly at Hudson.

"Grace and Hudson to see Aunt Emily and you are?"

The woman held up both hands. "Lucia. I'm helping Maria until Miss Emily is back on her feet."

Grace laughed. "That will be in no time at all." As soon as they entered the foyer, Grace saw Shelby carrying a tray that looked like dinner on it. Grace held up her hand and waved to her.

"We're in here," Aunt Emily said from the drawing room overlooking the Atlantic.

Grace inhaled the smell of ocean, seaweed and saltwater. "The smell of salty air will never stop amazing me. Every time I walk through that front door, it brings a smile to my heart." She bent down and hugged Aunt Emily. "How are you feeling?"

"Like a million bucks," Aunt Emily said then asked Shelby to set the tray down. "She needs to go back to the beach and start snapping more pictures. She won't let me go to the bathroom by myself."

"Stop," Shelby said as she shook her head. "I promised David I would take care of you."

Grace turned around looking for Hudson. Sounding as if

she was having a moment of panic, she called out his name. "Hudson—"

Hudson entered holding a gift bag filled with coloring books, puzzles and a new Lego. "Mommy look what Aunt Emily gave me." Then he pointed to Maria and said, "Maria said I can play with everything when I come to visit Aunt Emily."

Grace looked at Maria and nodded approvingly. "Ahh, thank you. Yes, because Aunt Emily is not allowed to walk on her foot for a whole week."

Aunt Emily held out her arms. "I can still get hugs from my favorite little guy though." Then she looked at Grace and told her she should have a dozen more children. "He's such a good boy. You should more children."

Grace smiled at the thought. "I would love to have a few more."

Aunt Emily reached out for Hudson to come closer. Hudson was careful to step to her good side before hugging her. "Thank you for my gifts." Then he sat down and told her about the little girl at day care.

Aunt Emily beamed with pride telling Hudson about David's first kiss. Grace felt tears sting her eyes thinking about Hudson's father. Wishing he were there to tell his son about his own first kiss. When emptiness took over, Grace stood up, looked out toward the ocean and said, "Okay, we need to get going. I just wanted to stop by and see if there is anything you need, but I see you're in good hands."

"Thank you for stopping by dear. Hudson, you may take your gifts home, but I hope you'll come see me again soon."

Hudson gave her one more hug before telling her. "I promise."

Once in the car, Grace told Hudson they had to stop by Aunt Ava's house.

"Does she have a surprise for me too?"

"Hudson, no. You don't always get a gift every time you visit those you love. We go see them because we love them not because we expect gifts from them." Grace looked in the rearview mirror and told him he was not alone. "All children love gifts. We need to appreciate them when they are given to us without expecting them. Okay?"

He nodded before asking, "Can I keep them in the bag until I see Aunt Emily again? She always helps me with my Lego's."

"Aww, see. You love Aunt Emily and appreciate her for loving you enough to teach you how to build and learn from her." When she winked at him, his frown turned to a bright smile.

When they got to Ava's house her car was not in the driveway. "Where can she be?"

"At the store, Mommy," Hudson said.

Grace called Ella. "She's not home. Are you sure she didn't tell you about going somewhere with Phillip?"

"On a workday? No, I would have scheduled someone to cover for her. Do you have Phillip's number? Maybe, we should call him."

"I don't," Grace replied and drove away. "I'm sure she has a good explanation."

"Yeah, okay," Ella said and then told Grace to have a good night.

"You, too," Grace said and hung up.

4

Ava sat outside Phillip's apartment devastated. She was hoping for an engagement ring, not a slap in the face. The sun was going down over Manhattan. Ava could see a bright yellow ball at the end of the row of tall buildings. In front of her, people were crossing the street; eating at café tables and talking as if everything was perfect in the world. As much as she wanted to go home, every time she put the car in drive... she broke down, sobbing.

When Phillip telephoned her to say he met with his parents to give them his news about the love of his life, Ava assumed he was finally going to propose to her. She was so excited the next morning she unexpectedly drove to his apartment, but when he told her about marrying his lover, Edward. Ava fainted.

"You should have called," Phillip said as he waved smelling salt under her nose.

Edward moved Phillip to the side. "Poor dear, are you okay?"

Ava could not believe her eyes. Edward could have been

her twin brother. Thin, blond, blue eyes and he even had a freckle under his right eye. She stared at him for a minute. "I can't believe this."

Edward helped her to a nearby chair. "Darling, how could you not know? I mean Phillip is a close friend... yes?"

Ava looked over at Phillip. Of course, he was moving about the apartment as if nothing at all had just happened. Phillip tucked his hair behind his ear. Raised his cup of espresso, took a sip and shook it off. "I never made you any promises. Ava, seriously, you should have called."

Ava wanted to throw something at him. "You are a son of a bitch. How could you?" She looked at Edward. "He didn't tell you we were dating?"

"Ava!" Phillip shouted. "Stop being so dramatic." He looked at Edward. "My mother asked me to accompany her to a few of her benefits." He wiped a bead of sweat from his forehead. "The woman is out of her mind for thinking it was anything other than—"

"You made love to me," she announced.

Edward crossed his arms over his chest. His eyes blinking. "When did you sleep with her, Phillip?"

"It doesn't matter. We're married now and I love you. Now stop with all this nonsense. Ava, you need to leave."

Phillip moved closer to where Ava was and put his arm around her shoulders. "She is not going anywhere until you tell me the truth. Besides, the poor woman is shaking." Edward went into the kitchen and poured a glass of water. He handed the glass and a box of tissues to Ava. Then he surprised everyone by sitting next to her and telling her that Phillip was pretending to be straight just to please his mother. "She's a wretched control freak who only cares about money and prestige." He patted Ava on her knee. "Trust me, sweetheart, I've been dealing with her for the past ten years." He shook his head. "I had to put the hammer down." He turned toward Phillip. "Or I was going back to California."

"How long have the two of you been together?" Ava asked in a voice so low Edward leaned in closer to make sure he heard her question.

Edward wiped his brow. "A whole decade as of May 1st. We met at UCLA, I hated him, he was so obnoxious. Telling me how I should dress, what shoes to wear and when I needed a haircut. He was so persistent I just knew he wasn't going to give up. Then one day, he took me to my favorite city in the world, and I knew I wanted to spend the rest of my life with him. I love New York. We went to a Broadway show, had dinner at Jean-Georges overlooking Central Park. And the next thing I knew we were buying a penthouse in Manhattan."

Ava took a sip of her water. Her hand was still shaking. Edward stood up and asked if he could get her something to eat. Ava shook her head and said she needed to use the bathroom. Edward helped her to her feet and showed her the way. Ava vomited for fifteen minutes, washed her face with cold water, sat down on the floor and cried. "How could I be so stupid?"

A moment later, she heard a knock on the door. "Ava, are you okay?" Phillip asked and then tapped on the door once more. "I'm sorry. I never meant to hurt you—"

"But you did," she said and got up. When she opened the door, both Edward and Phillip were standing in the hallway.

Edward offered her a helping hand. She reached for Edward's hand and said, "Thank you for being so kind to me." Then she turned toward Phillip. "You should have been honest with me." Her eyes filled up fast. "I fell in love with you." She wiped away her tears with the back of her hand. "I came here thinking you were going to ask me to marry you." She shook her head. When she reached up for the door jam, Edward wrapped his arm around her.

Ava kissed him on the cheek. "You are such a nice person. You deserve better. Thank you for your honesty." She walked out to the living area, bent down, picked up her pocketbook and walked out the door. As soon as she got in her car, she cried. "What am I going to tell everyone? They will never believe me." She looked up at the building. "I hate you so much. You're a no-good bastard." After sitting in her car for more than an hour, Ava found the courage to drive home. She knew Ella would be furious with her for not opening the store and she knew Grace would ask a thousand questions as to why she would drive all the way to the city without telling anyone.

As soon as she reached her house, she checked her cell phone. Both Grace and Ella left numerous messages. Ava took a deep breath, opened the car door and went inside the house. She made herself a cup of tea but never drank it. Instead, she poured herself a glass of vodka and after three glasses, she fell asleep on the couch. The next morning, she could hardly move, her head was throbbing, somehow, she made her way to the shower without falling. At eight-thirty, Ava opened the door to the store. She sent a group text telling Grace and Ella that she would explain her disappearance later that day. "I'm at the store. I will call you both this afternoon."

Immediately after Grace dropped Hudson off at day care, she went straight to the store to see Ava.

Ava was sitting behind the counter reading Grace's note when she heard the bell ring on the front door. Tears started streaming down her face. Grace stopped at the door and turned the sign to CLOSED. She walked up to Ava and hugged her. "It's okay. I'm here."

They sat on the floor behind the register. Grace rocked Ava in her arms as she listened to Ava explain every detail. "I had no idea," Ava cried.

Grace leaned back, looked Ava in her eyes and said, "God will send you your soulmate. A better person. Someone who deserves your crazy, wild, ass." They both laughed.

"Ella is going to take the store from me," Ava cried.

"No, she's not," Grace said as she moved a strand of hair out of Ava's eyes. "Ella loves you more than she does any damn store."

Ava smiled a little as she thanked Grace. "Thank you for covering for me."

"Any time. Just don's scare us like that again. If you need a day off, let one of us know. Okay?"

Ava nodded. "Do you really think there is someone out there waiting for me? For us?"

Grace took in a deep breath before replying, "I hope so." She tapped Ava on the head and told her she would stay with her and help run the store. When they saw two women looking in the front window, Grace waved to them. "I forgot I turned the sign." She walked toward the door and motioned for the women to give her a second. "Sorry about that. Come on in." Grace turned the sign back to OPEN, then she sent Ella a quick text. "I'm with Ava. She's okay. Please wait for my call. Talk soon."

At noontime, Grace and Ava called Ella to explain what had happened.

"Oh, Ava. I am so sorry. He didn't deserve you. You'll find a better a love, I promise."

5

May brought more and more people to the beach. Everywhere David looked they were setting up umbrellas, opening blankets and rubbing lotion on their bodies. In the background he could hear the weather person calling for sunshine and a gentle breeze coming up from the south. He sipped his coffee, watching a gorgeous sailboat cruise by. As much as he wanted to head up to the cabin, he knew he needed to stay close to Aunt Emily. He wanted to make sure she had everything she needed. He was glad their housekeeper, Maria hired a full-time house manager for Aunt Emily. Lucia did everything except clean. From getting the mail to serving meals, she was eager to do whatever it took to keep Aunt Emily happy. Because as soon as she got her boot off, it was back to traveling, meetings in upstate New York and the occasional trip to New York City to meet with her publisher.

David set his cup in the dishwasher, turned off the lamp in the living room and headed over to his aunt's house. He walked in holding a bag of bagels, cream cheese, smoked salmon and a jar of capers. He heard women laughing in the kitchen. Shelby and three other women were making plans for Aunt Emily's book launch celebration.

"Hey," Shelby said as David entered the kitchen. "Have you met Aunt Emily's assistant, social media manager and public relations person yet?"

David extended his hand to each of them. "No, I don't believe I have. It's nice to meet all of you. What are you working on?"

Aunt Emily's assistant stood up and explained. "We're working on her pre-launch campaign before her cookbook becomes available in September. Basically, we are going over every detail to make sure everything is in order."

"Sounds good and where is my favorite chef?"

Shelby pointed to the back patio. "She's in a Zoom meeting with her publisher." She smiled and raised a brow. "I will be taking all of the photos for the event." She tilted her head to the left. "I'm so excited to be on her street team."

David looked down at the stack of paperwork. "I'll wait for her in the sitting room. I want to ask her for her opinion."

Shelby looked past everyone at Lucia. "She is amazing. Aunt Emily loves her. She hired her full time. Honestly, she spoils Aunt Emily and me. She made us a chicken tortilla soup that was to die for." She waved a hand at him. "You have to try it."

David went into the sitting room, picked up the newspaper and read the first three pages before Aunt Emily came into the room. He set the paper down and got up to assist her, but she brushed his hand away. "Why aren't you up at the cabin fishing?"

David sat back down. "I wanted to see if you needed anything and ask your opinion about something."

Aunt Emily moved closer to David, picked up her glass

of water and took a sip. Before setting it back down, she said, "I'm doing great. I have plenty of help. You don't have to worry about me. I appreciate it, but I am fine." She winked at him. "Honestly, now tell me what's on your mind."

David blew out a long breath. "I'm thinking about buying a piece of land and building a few tiny houses for the homeless."

Aunt Emily allowed a smile to rise naturally. Then she did a double take outside. "The ocean is calm today, not a whitecap to be found. Simply gorgeous outside, one might say it's a perfect day and yet so many people will never see the beauty in the world because they are hurting. They have no roof over their heads, food on their tables or clean clothes to wear." She bowed her head before looking up at him. "David, you make me proud every day. You will not stop until you make sure every person in Point Judith is fed and—"

"Safe," he said before she could say another word. "So, you think I should give it a shot?"

"Absolutely," she said.

David hugged her. "I'm glad you have everyone around you. They're all nice and they seem to care a lot about you. If you're good, I'd like to go to the cabin for a few days and work on my idea."

"I have a great team. They traveled from New York and New Jersey to assist me. And don't take this the wrong way, but, if I have Lucia... I don't need anyone else."

David kissed her on the cheek and said he would call her every day. "I'll check in on you tomorrow." He said goodbye to everyone else and headed up to the cabin.

As soon as David got to the cabin, he called Grace to let her know the beach house was available if she wanted to take Hudson swimming. "Hey, I'm up at the cabin for the next few days, if you want to use the beach house go right ahead."

"Ahh, thanks. I just might. You don't mind if I invite Ava to stay with me, do you?"

"Not at all. Give her my love and tell her to say hi to Phillip."

Grace explained Ava's situation to David. "Phillip and Ava broke up. She's devastated."

"I'm sorry to hear that. If the two of you need anything let me know."

"Hey, I'll check in on Aunt Emily for you while you're away."

David laughed. "Grace, I'm only a half hour away. She's fine. Shelby is with her, in fact her entire entourage is there and, she hired a full-time house manager."

Grace echoed David's laugh. "That's our Aunt Emily. Okay, see you soon."

David poured himself a brandy, sat down and logged onto the computer. He found the perfect piece of land. He wished he could tell Grace and perhaps ask for her help, but for now he wanted to keep it a secret; at least until he had most of the details in place. Next, he looked at small houses. One company offered kits, another sold what looked to be sheds. David considered his options. He knew what he was looking for, he just had to keep searching. "Wow," he said when he discovered a builder specializing in "tiny houses" with two floor plans that would work perfectly for David's community. One house offered a great room, kitchen, bedroom, bathroom and a laundry room—perfect for a single person. The other plan would work for a couple or two individuals. "I'm sure a lot of women would like a companion." That plan offered the same as the other house except it had two bedrooms and a bath and a half. David was pleased to see both houses offered a covered front porch and a rear patio.

He called the builder and explained what he was trying to do. The man said he would cut him a good price and be willing to deliver them for free. David wrote down his name, number and the quote for the houses.

By the time David finished looking it was almost seven o'clock, the sun was going down over the lake and he was starving. He felt like celebrating so he ordered a pizza from Moussaka Pizzeria. "Extra meatballs, eggplant and cheese. Thanks, I'll meet you at the gate." David hung up the phone and went out to the garage. He got in the Polaris Ranger 1500, turned on the radio and listened to The Drifters. As soon as he heard "Under The Boardwalk" he cranked up the volume. One thing was for sure, David never changed the channel in the Ranger, Henry loved the oldies. "Huh, maybe I should see if Shelby and Henry want to go out on a date." He laughed aloud thinking about Henry never leaving the gatehouse or the property for that matter. David decided to leave things alone. Henry was his friend and a damn good property manager.

David pressed the button to open the gate in time to receive his dinner. "Thank you."

"Thanks for the tip," the driver said in return.

The next song had David wondering if it were true. "Is there really a sea of love?" Then, the radio announcer said there was a volleyball tournament going on next weekend at Salty Brine Beach. "I'm glad I won't be there for that," David said, and parked the Ranger back in the garage.

After dinner, David grabbed a book, sat down on the front porch and read for an hour. He set the book down and decided it was time to move forward.

The next morning, David drove into town, he parked his

Tahoe across the street from the Auntie Em's soup kitchen. The line was longer than the last time he visited. He shook his head in disbelief. "I have to do more." He reached for his cellphone called Grace and told her his plans. "I looked at a few parcels. Can you check them out and get back to me by the end of the day?"

"Send me the addresses and I will get right to work on it. Hey, I'll do whatever I can to make this plan happen."

David stopped by Aunt Emily's to check on her and to tell her he had Grace working on a few locations. "Grace has a short list of properties and if I know Grace, she'll nail one of them down."

"I'm excited for you. The thought of you and Grace working together again is—"

"Aunt Emily, stop. Grace is a friend and that is all she is." David tilted his head and reminded her that Grace was still not over losing Hudson's father. "I respect her for who she is, for giving herself time to heal and for doing a remarkable job raising their son, but I am not interested."

"She deserves a good man in her life, and I happen to know she wants more children."

David got up, leaned over and kissed her on the forehead. "I'll call you tomorrow and let you know if we're successful."

David was driving down Route 108 when his cell buzzed. He pulled over and took the call. "Hey, any luck?"

Grace chuckled. "David, I'm better than lucky. I'm so good, I have three lots for you to look at. Do you want me to pick you up or do you want to drive?"

"I'm just heading into town. I can pick you up at your house in five minutes."

"Great, let me call the day care and ask if Hudson can

stay for the after-school activities. I need to be back by six to get him."

"Sounds good and hey, thanks." When David pulled up to Grace's house she was waiting for him at the end of the driveway, folder in hand, wearing her signature crimson smile. She got in the Tahoe, buckled up and rubbed her hands together.

"I have a good feeling about two of the lots. The other realtor told me they are both eager to sell, which means I should be able to get the price down for you." She looked at him and told him to take US 1 north. "Take one to I95 to 295 north, then the first parcel is a few miles down the road."

"I'd like to stay under one million if I can. I'll have a lot to do before the first house is delivered."

"What's first on the list?" Grace asked and then told him his exit was up ahead.

"Zoning laws are always a priority, then permits, hopefully approvals and if I'm lucky the perk test comes back good, and only then we can start clearing the land." He rubbed his neck before adding. "The soil will need to be tested to ensure there's no contamination anywhere."

"And then what?" she asked wondering if she could help.

"We start working on utilities, driveways and hopefully the new houses get delivered before next summer."

"I'm so glad I get to be a part of it," she said.

David and Grace looked at all three lots. The first one offered sixty-six acres of raw land, but the price tag on that lot was a little over one million and the owner was not coming down on his price. The second lot was perfect—it had eighty-one acres and was under seven-hundred-thousand-dollars, but it had a pending offer on it. Next, they looked at a parcel with one-hundred and thirty-six acres for a little over a million dollars. "Let me put in an offer and see if they take it," Grace said feeling confident. "The listing agent said she was ready to sell and get away from paying any more taxes."

"Wow, a hundred and thirty-six acres would give me plenty of room to do what I want to do and then some."

Grace stood near the Tahoe, looked out at the land and said, "I may have a grocery store willing to invest in your idea."

David could see her wheels turning. "I never thought about it that way. Do you think we can get a drug store, maybe even an eatery that would be willing to get involved?"

"David, with your charm and vision... why not?" She opened the car door and told him she needed to get back. "Let's go, I have to pick Hudson up."

"Hey, why don't I take us all out for pizza?"

"Any time I don't have to cook, is fine by me," she said smiling.

The owner of On Point Pizza was more than pleased to hear about David's new venture. "Definitely, keep me posted," he said.

David shook his hand and told him he would offer him free rent for the first year. "Listen, these people deserve the best. They've suffered enough and if we can make their lives a little more enjoyable—"

"Hell yeah," Grace said. "I'm glad we mentioned it to you."

"Hey, a friend of mine has the café, she has the best coffee and comfort food around. I know she would be willing to expand."

The look on David's face was priceless. He bent down, picked Hudson up, twirled him in a full circle and said,

"Your Mommy is a genius." He extended his hand out to the owner one more time. "Thanks, again."

"Let's stop at the drug store. Maybe, they would like the opportunity to be a part of this," Grace said as she accepted the pizza box with their leftovers.

When Hudson yawned, David said, "I think someone is a little tired. We can go another day. I better be getting the two of you, home."

Grace patted Hudson on his head. "Did you have a busy day today?"

"We played outside all day," he replied and climbed in the booster seat. "Is Uncle David coming to our house?"

"No, sorry. I'm going to drop you off and then get going, but I'll see you another day," David said as he started the vehicle; but when he looked in the rear-view-mirror and saw Hudson make a sad face he asked him, "Hudson, are you... okay?"

"You promised me you would read The Little Digger to me? You gave it to me. Remember?"

"I did for your birthday, right? Okay, then I guess I better come in and read you a bedtime story."

After David read to Hudson, he joined Grace in the living room. She put her book down and asked him if he wanted a cup of tea or a shot of bourbon.

"You know what? A bourbon sounds good right about now." He sat down in the recliner. He watched her pour two glasses and thought. I hope she finds love again. She's such a sweet, warm and tenderhearted woman.

Grace tapped her glass to his. "Cheers. Here's to both of our dreams coming true."

race dropped Hudson off at day care and headed for the beach. She used her key to go inside and bumped right into David's housekeeper. "Maria, I'm sorry, I forgot you still clean even though David is up to the cabin. How are you?"

"I'm good, Miss Grace and you?"

"I just came in to use the bathroom and then I'm going for a nice long walk down the beach, so I'll be out of your way in just a minute."

"No worries. I like seeing you and David together." She smiled and raised a brow. "Will he be joining you?"

Grace laughed, knowing she too was hopeful the two of them would get together. "No, he's working on a new project up at the cabin for the next few days."

Grace walked down the beach toward Aunt Carrie's Restaurant. Up ahead, she saw a man that looked just like Red, but it wasn't him. She wondered how Red was doing and if she could convince him to move to David's new community. When she bent down to pick up a shell, she could hear a man calling for his children to join him in the water. His wife kept telling him it was too cold for them. Grace smiled at the woman and waved to the three children building a sandcastle. When she rubbed her arms several times, one of the girls nodded in agreement.

Grace continued her trek. For a moment, she imagined what life would be like if she and David did get together. After all, he was every woman's dream—handsome, respectful, kind and he was sweet on the eye. Grace felt her face getting warm. She glanced up at the sun and a warm feeling came over her. She missed being in love, with a man and she longed for companionship. Reading children's stories every night was great for Hudson, but she needed romance in her life and not the kind you get from a book. Grace blinked away tears that clouded her eyes. "I miss you so much," she said, sniffling and continued walking down the beach. She stopped, turned around and waved when she heard her name being called.

"I thought that was you," Red said.

She gave him a hug. "I was just thinking about you. How have you been?"

"I'm doing okay for an old man."

"Stop," she said and then asked if he wanted to escort her. "Would you like to go to lunch with me? I could use a friend right now."

Right before he called out to her, he saw her crying. He too shed a tear that morning. He closed his eyes in a long blink. His eyes still burning as his heart ached thinking about the past. When he didn't answer her right away, she asked again.

"I'm going to Aunt Carries, we can sit outside and watch the waves crash on the shore. I would love it if—"

A long, almost uncomfortable silence hummed between

them, his eyes locked on hers. Red looked at her for a moment longer before saying, "I would like that."

"Great," Grace said and looped her arm through his. The wind tousled her hair. She went to move it, but Red had already tucked it behind her ear. She smiled at the sheepish look on his face. "Have you ever known a woman who wanted a baby so badly her heart ached?"

Red stopped walking for a second. "You don't need a man to have a baby. These days, you can buy a man's sperm."

Grace offered a gentle smile. Her cheeks still red. She wasn't sure if it was from the sun or from her thinking about David. Her eyes widened. "I almost went that route once. I think I'm ready to share my life with someone. Red, my heart is ready for love."

"You're a very beautiful woman. Now that your heart is open, I am sure love will find you." Red opened the door for her to go inside just as a few raindrops started falling.

"We'll sit inside until it stops," she said.

Red nodded in agreement. When he went to pay, Grace slid a fifty toward the cashier. "I invited you," she said.

"Only if you allow me to buy the ice cream," he said in return.

She blushed telling him David had a freezer full of homemade strawberry ice cream. "He makes the best," she said as they sat down at the corner table. Grace and Red chatted for an hour enjoying each other's company. "Red, can I ask you something?"

Red normally avoids those questions, but he liked Grace. He swallowed before answering her. "Yes."

"How old are you?"

Red laughed aloud. "For a minute there I thought you were going to ask me—"

"For your sperm?" She said laughing loud enough for the entire room to hear her.

Red joined in her laughter. "No, no," he said and sat back in his chair. "I thought you were going to ask me why I am homeless. It's the first question everyone asks when they see me." Red wiped the corners of his mouth with his knuckle. "I'm forty-nine."

"I would never judge anyone. You seem to be content with your life." Grace's eyes opened wide. "Red, can I share a little secret with you?" She didn't wait for his response. She told him about David's plans. "In addition to the soup kitchen, he wants to help people find a safe place to live."

"He's a very generous young man. Grace, I want you to know something about me. I chose this life for a reason. You don't have to agree with me, but it's how it is."

"Red, you're my friend. I stand by you in all that you do. Through the storm and in the sunlight. We're friends for life." She chuckled. "Besides, I may need your sperm if I can't find a man."

Red picked up their plates, empty water bottles and put everything in the garbage can on their way out. When he held the door open for her, she smiled and said, "Thank you." Then she pointed toward two empty Adirondack chairs. "It stopped raining, do you have time to sit for a while longer?"

Red pondered her invitation for a second. "For you I have all day."

They sat down and watched the calm water drift in and out. "I always liked sitting by the ocean after a good rain shower," he said.

"Why is that?" she asked as she sat down next to him.

"Each drop of rain produces a vortex ring which, on descending into the water, transfers momentum from the surface layers to the underneath layers, thus reducing the relative motion of the layers." He held out his right hand. "Calmness."

She studied his face for second. "You don't have to answer this, but were you ever married?"

"Once," he said, sat up and leaned forward as if he were getting up to leave.

Grace wanted to ask him if he ever had children of his own, but she decided to go slow with Red, she enjoyed his company and friendship more than anything else. She told him about Hudson and how he died weeks before their wedding. How David helped her get through the toughest time in her life. "I adore David, he's like the brother I never had. As great of a guy as he is—"

Red touched her on her arm. "Trust your instincts. You'll recognize love when you see him."

"Red, when Hudson died, I thought I would never want another man in my life." She looked out at the ocean. Lost in the moment.

Red sat quietly next to her. He knew exactly how she felt. He too lost the love of his life. "A broken heart is the worst, it's like having broken ribs, nobody can see it, but it hurts every time you breathe."

7

The next day, Grace met a deckhand at day care. Her eyes fell to his lips, full, red, sweetly curved.

"Hi, I'm Dylan and this is my son, Devon."

Grace bent down and asked Devon if he enjoyed coming to day care. "Are you having as much fun at day care as Hudson?"

"Hudson is my best friend; we play together outside."

Hudson agreed with Devon telling his mother all about the sand box. Mommy, we both love playing in the boat making sandcastles."

"Hudson is the captain and I'm the deckhand," Devon said as he looked up at his father.

Dylan laughed telling Grace that he was a deckhand on one of the fishing boats. "I work on The Super Squirrel. I would love to take the two of you out sometime. Devon has a great time. He enjoys watching the seagulls dive for scraps."

"Scraps?" Graced asked wondering if he was referring to garbage.

"Oh, sorry. Chum—fish, cut up into small pieces and thrown from the boat to attract larger fish."

Grace nodded approvingly as she listened to Dylan tell Hudson how sea gulls dive in both fresh and salt water. "Sea gulls have a special pair of glands right above their eyes which are specifically designed to flush the salt from their systems through openings in the bill."

"Mommy, can we go? Please?" Hudson said as he tugged on her hand.

She was impressed with both Dylan and Devon. "We would love to go fishing one day."

"Great," Dylan replied and then asked if they had plans for the weekend. "How does Saturday morning sound?"

"Mommy, can we?" Hudson asked with a grin of approval.

"Okay. What time should we meet you?"

Dylan explained where the boat was docked and told her to be there by eight. "You don't have to bring anything, I'll take care of the food, drinks and sun block. Oh, you might want to take Dramamine." He held up his pointer finger. "I'll walk you to your car and give you some chewable Dramamine safe for children."

Grace thanked Dylan and told him about fishing one other time. "I went deep sea fishing with a friend of mine, he's friends with Russ Benn."

"Ahh, the Seven B's. Yes, Russ is a great guy. One of the masters." Dylan held his hand out to her. "Grace, I'm glad I ran into you. I usually drop Devon off by seven, but today I'm in charge of picking up all the chum, so I came later than normal."

They both laughed. Grace snorted, held her hand up to her mouth and said, "Yeah, that's all you. I'll see you tomorrow."

His instant smile gave her a jolt of hope for the future. Grace got in her car and drove straight to the store to tell Ava about her chance meeting, but when she parked the car in front of The Lighthouse Inn, she drove away. As soon as she got home, she texted Ella to see if she had a minute to talk. "Hey, got a minute?"

Instead of texting back, Ella called her. "Yes, what's up?"

"Oh, my heart. I am going fishing tomorrow with a dreamboat." Sounding silly, she added. "Ella, he has a strong jaw, head full of dark hair, smiling eyes, and he was so charismatic, I had to say yes." The thought washed over Grace like a cool waft of water on a hot summer day.

"Oh, Grace. I am so happy for you. Tell me more. Every detail. How and where did you meet him?"

"At day care. His son is the same age as Hudson. We're meeting him and his son, Devon tomorrow to go fishing for the day."

Silence on the other end of the line.

"Ella—"

"I'm here. He has a son. Does he also have a girlfriend or a wife?"

Grace's heart sank. "I never thought about that. Shit, shit, shit." She looked up at the sun, it was beaming in the kitchen window making it even hotter. She opened the window as a breeze passed by, along with a soft, musky smell. "It's Red's fault. He told me I would meet someone. He said as soon as I open my heart... love would find me. I can't believe I fell for it."

"So, the news about your heart is good, but I think you should ask him if he's married," Ella said. "Before you get your hopes up."

"We didn't exchange numbers." Grace leaned up against

the counter feeling like a fool for calling. "I'm sorry, I should have asked him before calling you and—"

"Hang on a minute. If I met Mr. Mc Dreamy, you would be the first person I would call. Hey, maybe it's too soon to tell Ava though."

"Yeah, I drove to the store to tell her but quickly turned back around."

Laughingly, Ella said, "So I was your second choice? I'm kidding. Was the store open?"

"Yes, and her car was there. In fact, she's there early. Right?"

"No, this week is inventory week. Good, I'm glad she's working it will keep her mind off that asshole. Who dates a woman knowing you are in love with a man?"

"Do you think I should stay home tomorrow? Because honestly, I'm not up for this... oh crap, I already told Hudson, and he's excited to be spending the day with his friend."

"I got it. Call the day care and ask one of the workers if the kid's mother ever picks him up or drops him off."

"I'll just go and if I find out he is married, I'll toss him overboard," Grace said offering a rueful laugh.

"Hey, I'll tell you what. You go to this damn wedding, and I'll go fishing."

"Oh yeah, you're going to a wedding where you won't know a soul. Maybe, Mr. Right will be there, and we can double date."

"Kiss my ass," Ella said and then added. "Hey, can you check on Ava this weekend? I called her last night, and she sounded a little too giddy for my blood."

"Of course. I'll swing over in a little while. Okay, bye."

After Grace picked Hudson up from day care she drove to the store to see Ava. When she got there several customers where shopping. Ava was assisting a woman trying to get her to try on a sun dresses. When Ava saw Grace, she turned her head quickly as if to say I'm busy, so Grace waved to her and mouthed the words, "I'll stop back." She sent Ella a text letting her know Ava was working and seemed fine. "The store is busy and so was Ava. Talk later, love you."

Ella texted her back. "Love and miss the two of you more every day."

When Ella stopped asking about David, Grace made a point to stop talking about him. She felt horrible for even mentioning Shelby to her.

That night before bedtime and the next morning, both she and Hudson took their dose of Dramamine. "Are you excited to go fishing on the big boat today?"

"Yes, and I even have a present for Devon."

"You do? What do you have?"

"I have a bag of French fries for him."

"Where on earth did you get the fries?"

"I saved them at lunchtime. Devon loves to feed the seagulls. He said when his mother was alive, she used to give him a bag to take with him every time he went to work with his father."

Grace's heart dropped. Her eyes filled up fast. She felt sorry for the little boy. "I'm sorry Devon doesn't have his mother any longer." She gave Hudson a hug. "You are such a good friend. I'm proud of you for thinking about Devon and making his day even more special."

Up ahead, Dylan and Devon stood waiting. Grace's pulse fluttered at the sweet hope on his face. He was handsome in an adorable way. When he reached for her hand to help her aboard, she let out a breath she didn't know she had been holding.

"Good morning, you two," Dylan said.

"Hi, this is for you," Hudson said as he handed the bag to Devon.

Devon smiled from ear to ear. "You remembered the story I told you. Daddy, look." He held the bag up.

Dylan went down on one knee and gave Hudson a nod of thanks and then he shook his hand. "You just made his day and mine. Thank you for doing that."

"You're welcome," Hudson said. "I told my mom the story, too."

Dylan smiled warmly at Grace. "I had planned to tell you at a later time."

Grace reach over and touched his arm. "It's okay. Today, is about catching fish, smiles and making long lasting memories. Right guys?"

For a moment, Dylan's expression changed to embarrassment. "I'm not very good at this kind of stuff, but when I saw you... I knew I had to meet you." His face was warm with perusal as he admitted seeing Grace a few days earlier. "I saw you dropping Hudson off last week and asked their teacher if you were single."

8

J uly 4th proved to be an exciting day, Dr. Ferris was hosting a barbecue and just down the road at 91 Point Judith Road fireworks were expected to start at dusk. Every neighbor from as far away as three miles was invited to the neighborhood block party. Grace helped him hire the caterers and the quartet. Audrain Hospitality offered a great menu, and they even provided the alcohol and floral arrangements—burgundy dahlia, white lily and blue hydrangea.

The party was scheduled to start at five and last until the firework display. From the oyster bar to the long tables featuring starters, salads stacked three tiers high sat under a large tent; everyone was guaranteed to have a great time.

Grace was happy when Dylan said he would attend the party with her. Hudson was over the moon excited his friend would be there to play with. "Remember, Dr. Ferris invited you because you are a very good little boy, so don't be getting into trouble with the girls."

"Mommy, stop. Aunt Emily said she has a surprise for

me, and I can play with it at the party." He gave her a pointed look. "I didn't ask her for a surprise. She asked me if I was going to the party and said she had a new toy I could play with in the sand."

Grace offered a shy grin. "Aunt Emily loves you so much. She can spoil you all she wants." She handed him his breakfast and asked him if he liked spending time with Devon and his father. "Does it make you happy being around Devon and his dad?"

"I like Dylan, he's nice to me and—"

"And what, Honey?"

"I saw you kiss Dylan. Do you like him?"

Grace blushed. "As far as that kiss goes, I was thanking him for taking us fishing and yes I like him very much."

Hudson smiled. "Then I like him too," Hudson announced and began eating his scrambled eggs.

Grace introduced Dylan and Devon to Dr. Ferris, Aunt Emily, David and to Ava. "This is Dylan and his son, Devon. We met at day care a few weeks ago."

David and Dr. Ferris shook Dylan's hand. Aunt Emily handed Hudson and Devon each a mesh bag filled with sand toys. Then she moved to one of the chaise lounges under the big umbrella.

The quartet played "Sea of Love" by Cat Power, and everyone started dancing in the sand. Couples held each other close. Dylan reached for Grace's hand. "Care to dance?"

"I'd love to." She offered a meek smile as she accepted his hand. A few seconds later, a surprising laugh rumbled out of her as she gave him a sideways glance. Her eyes softened as she stared back at him. Her pulse skittered when she drew in a breath.

Dylan whispered in her ear. "You can't hide happiness. I like being here with you."

Grace rested her head on Dylan's shoulder. "I enjoy being with you too."

When the next song started, Dylan twirled Grace around before pulling her in closer.

Aunt Emily sat there until she had enough. She walked up to David and handed him a cold Corona. "David. Still putting a pickle in your beer?" she asked as she handed it to him. She chuckled as she called out his name again. "David?"

"Yes, thank you," he said and accepted the beverage.

"I found the perfect woman for you."

"Not interested," he said and took a sip.

"David, she's beautiful, smart and she has her own money."

"Go away, Aunt Emily. I'm not looking for—"

Interrupting him, she asked, "Are you sure?" Then she patted him on his back. "I'd be happy to introduce you to her."

"I know what I want and it's not one of Taylor's high-class friends."

"Okay, and what exactly are you looking for?" She drank from her glass and then held it up waiting.

He laughed, knowing his aunt would not stop until he told her. "I want someone who is down to earth." He looked up again. "A natural beauty, not some made up fancy—"

"David are you sure you don't want me to introduce the two of you. I mean after all you have been staring at her all afternoon." Aunt Emily purposely started to walk away leaving him to chase after her.

"Wait a second you. Come back here. And no, I have not

been staring at anyone." His brows drew together. "Umm, who are you talking about?"

First Aunt Emily chuckled, then she gave a nod toward the woman sitting in the beach chair next to Ava. The two women were sipping Cotes de Provence Rose. They even had their very own ice bucket to keep the wine cold.

David squinted against the sun, which glared blindingly on the water. "Please don't say Ava?"

"Nope," she replied and then tossed a fond smile over her shoulder. "I'm referring to the brunette that you can't keep your eyes off. She's one of my favorite writers. I attended one of her book signings last year at The Strand in New York."

David offered a strain smile. "Was I really staring at her?"

"Don't worry, I was the only person looking at you looking at her," she said with a cheeky smile. "So... do you want to know more or should I just—"

David put his hand on her shoulder. "What else do you know?" He asked as he looked one more time at how her floral halter dress complemented her tanned, slender shoulders perfectly.

Aunt Emily explained that she rented a house a few doors down from Dr. Ferris. "She's writing a new beach read series."

The first thought David had was... she's only here for a short time. "I'm not looking for a summer romance."

"Ahh, I knew you would say that. Aren't you lucky. She's here for a year, now go work your magic. Her name is Judith Ann. Look her up." Once again, she went to walk away, but David stopped her.

"Aunt Emily, magic has nothing to do with anything.

When the time is right, I will meet someone who shares my values. Someone who enjoys sipping coffee before the sun comes up, who isn't afraid to walk in the rain. I'm looking for a princess."

"Huh," she said. "You left out kissing under moonlit skies."

He scratched the side of his head. "Fine, are you going to introduce me or do I have to ask Ava to do the honors?"

Aunt Emily nodded slowly. "Haha, oh one more thing, I heard her tell one of the other guests, she's looking for someone to show her around." Emily winked. "Follow me."

Aunt Emily and David walked up to Ava and Judith Ann. "Hello, Ava. Judith Ann, I'd like to introduce you to my nephew, David."

Ava sat up, turned to face them, dropped her wine glass in the sand, rolled out of her chair and fell flat on her face.

David bent down and picked her up. "Ava, I think you've had a little too much to drink." Her eyes were a glare of ice, her cheeks redder than the sun on a hot summer day. David looked at Judith Ann and said, "Judith, it's nice to meet you. I'd be happy to show you around, but it's not happening today. Ava, I'm taking you back to my place so you can sleep this off." He was carrying her toward his house when Grace noticed him. She ran after them, hollering for Dylan to please keep an eye on the boys.

A moment later, Grace caught up to David. "What happened? Is she okay?"

Ava was passed out in David's arms. "Ava may have had a little too much to drink."

When they arrived at David's house, Grace assisted David by opening the gate and the door upstairs. Grace followed David into the bedroom. "I'll get a cool washcloth for her head," Grace said and went into the bathroom. When she got back to the bedroom, Ava looked pale.

A moment later, Ava said she felt sick. David picked her up and carried her to the bathroom. David stood in the doorway listening to Grace scold Ava for drinking so much. "No man is worth getting this drunk over."

9

M onday morning, Ava was at the store when Grace arrived. It was only ten o'clock and she appeared drunk. "Are you drinking?" Grace said impulsively.

Ava lifted her mug in a mock toast. "Cheers."

Grace walked over to her, took the mug from her and sniffed it. Then she lifted the lid. "Is that vodka?" Grace moved closer to the bathroom, stopped and told Ava to lock the front door. "Go and lock the door, right now." Then she proceeded to dump the contents down the drain. When she returned, Ava was still standing in the same spot. Grace went over, turned the sign to CLOSED and locked the door. She dialed Ella's number, put the cellphone speaker on and told her they had a problem on their hands. "I'm at the store. You're not going to believe this, but Ava is drunk."

"WHAT?" Ella shouted for the world to hear. "Ava, what is wrong with you?"

Grace raised her brows, looking at Ava waiting for her to explain herself, but when she sat on the floor and started to cry, Grace had tears in her eyes as she explained to Ella that

Ava was not dealing with the whole Phillip situation, well. "She's not going to make it on her own. I think she needs—"

"Me?" Ella said in a soft voice. "I'm on my way. Ava, you listen to me." Ella started to cry. "We'll get through this. You're not alone. Grace, I'm on my way." Then she hung up the phone.

Grace's jaw tightened as she nodded to Ava. "What are you doing to yourself? Why would you throw everything away for a man like Phillip?" She sat down on the floor and held Ava in her arms. "You wanted to move to Point Judith, you said you could handle running the store on your own." Grace looked into Ava's eyes. "This was your dream. Your customers love you. Oh, Ava, what am I to do with you?" Once again, Grace's jaw muscles flex and her eyes were lost in thought as she fervently said, "I can't lose you, too."

Ava cleared her throat before saying, "I don't want to live anymore."

"First of all," Grace said, "you're lying, and I can tell." Then she shot Ava a pointed look, brow arched as she tapped Ava on the nose. "You're the strongest, feistiest woman I know. Fashion is in your blood. Never mind, you've had more men than I've had bras. So, what the hell is really going on here?"

Ava swallowed every excuse and reason. Then she pulled back a little as her eyes searched for the bottle she left on the floor when she heard Grace calling her name. Grace brushed Ava's hair back. They sat on the floor for a few minutes longer before Grace said, "We better get you cleaned up before Ella gets here."

"I'm fine. Hey, can you go out to my car and grab my pocketbook?"

Grace studied her face for a moment before saying, "Sure, first, let me help you to your feet." When Grace stood

Ava up, she noticed Ava's pocketbook sitting on the counter next to the cash register. She walked over to the door and pretended to go to Ava's car, but instead Grace stood outside looking in the window watching Ava. Grace gasped when she saw Ava pick up the bottle and empty it entirely. Ava must have downed six ounces all at once. Grace ran back inside, took Ava by the arm with one hand and grabbed the empty bottle with her other hand.

Ava laughed uncontrollably. Her eyes slide open, fluttered and then close again. Her voice cracked when she announced she had to use the bathroom. "I have to pee."

Grace helped her to the bathroom. Ava tried to close the door behind her, but Grace put her foot out. When Ava did not sit down on the toilet, Grace entered the bathroom, bent down and open the two doors under the sink. Grace grabbed the new bottle of vodka, opened it and poured every drop down the sink. Ava began to cry. "Please give it to me."

"NO," Grace shouted. Grace sat Ava down on the toilet and told her to go to the bathroom, but it was too late, Ava had already urinated all over herself. "Ava, oh my gosh. Stand up." Grace pulled her pants and her panties down, tossed them in the sink and told Ava not to move. She went out to the front room and grabbed a long skirt. When she went back into the bathroom, Ava was passed out on the floor.

Grace slid the skirt up and on her, put the toilet seat down and closely watched Ava. When her cellphone rang, she immediately answered it on the first ring. "Hey," Grace said to Ella.

"I just turned onto Great Island Road. How is she?"

Grace held back her tears. "I'm not going to lie to you, she's a mess. You still have your key, right?"

"Yeah, where are you?"

"We're in the bathroom. She's out cold." Grace started to cry. "She wet herself. Ella, what are we going to do?"

"Breathe, Grace. I'll be there before you know it."

Ella parked her car next to Grace's and went inside. She stood outside the bathroom with tears in her eyes. Grace was sitting on the floor with Ava's head on her lap. When Grace saw Ella, she held up one finger and whispered, "She's drinking vodka straight out of the bottle."

Ella motioned for Grace to come out to the front room. Then she took hold of a towel, rolled it up, bent down and put it under Ava's head. Ella and Grace stood outside the bathroom trying to come up with a plan. "I can't have her running the store. Not like this," Ella said.

"What are you going to do?"

Ella shook her head. "I'll have to stay here until I can find someone to run the place in her absence."

"Wait. Where is she going?"

"Grace, look at her. She needs help. I called a friend of mine and she suggested we put her in rehab where she can get the help she needs." Ella rubbed her forehead before adding, "I'll pay for it. They have a good therapist on staff. My friend used to work with her at Sharon Hospital, now she's at High Watch Recovery Center. A lot of celebrities go there. They have a ninety-nine-percent success rate."

Grace snapped her neck to look at Ella. "Who falls into the one-percentile?"

Ella offered a grim face. "Some people don't make it. They die." She held her hand up like a stop sign. "She is not that bad and that's why we're going to get her into this clinic as soon as a bed opens up."

"Great, and in the meantime, what are we supposed to do with—"

They both heard Ava moan. Together, they stood in the doorway, watching Ava hug the bowl. Ella stopped Grace from going in. "Let her go. She needs to learn to stand on her own two feet."

When Ava heard Ella's voice her head dropped to the rim of the toilet seat.

For the next several days, Ella kept a close eye on Ava. Living with her, going to work every day and interviewing a new woman to run the store in Ava's absence. "Ava, celebrities will be there. You can introduce them to your clothing lines. I insist you go. I promise you; I will come and see you as soon as it is allowed."

"How long do I have to go?" Ava cried.

"For as long as you need," Ella said. "Ava, it's nestled in three-hundred wooded acres. They offer state-of-the-art treatment, and I know one of the people who works there, she'll take good care of you."

"I promise, I won't drink anymore. I'll—"

"No, I'm not backing down. Not this time. You are my business partner, my best friend, I need you more than you know. You're going and that's it."

A long dreadful hour went by. Ava started feeling sick. "I'm going to go to lunch with my friend, do you want me to bring you back anything?"

Ella looked at her before asking her. "Who are you going with?"

"My friend," Ava said and turned her back. She moved a pair of pants to a different spot, walked over closer to the door and said, "She's here. I'll be back in a few minutes."

Ella gave the girl one look and said, "No, you're not going anywhere with her. I don't know her and I don't like the looks of her."

"Ella," Ava protested. "Who the fuck are you to say that?"

Ella crossed her arms over her chest. "I just told you. I am your business partner and you are not going anywhere with that woman." Ella moved closer to the front door. She opened the door and told the woman Ava was busy. "We're a little busy right now, maybe another day."

The woman stepped inside and gave Ava a quick hug. "It's okay, we can go tomorrow."

Ava shrugged. "Yeah, okay. Thanks."

For the rest of the day, Ava kept her distance from Ella. When Grace called the store, Ava heard Ella tell her about not letting her leave her sight.

At nine o'clock, Ella went into Ava's bedroom and found her on the floor, eyes rolled back in her head, foaming at the mouth. Ava was lying there with no top on. She was white as a ghost. Ella dialed 911, held Ava in her arms and waited for the ambulance to arrive. As soon as they got there, they used Narcan. But before the ambulance could reach the hospital, Ava had a seizure.

Once Ella got to the emergency room, and the doctors took over, she called Grace to let her know where they were. "I don't know what happened. I think that woman slipped her drugs."

"I'm not waking my son up to bring him to—"

"No, no," Ella said. "I've got this. I'll stop by as soon as I know she is okay. I'm sure they're going to keep her overnight."

"Okay, I'll wait up for you. Text me when you leave the hospital," Grace said and hung the phone up.

At eleven o'clock a doctor advised Ella of Ava's condition. "She's lucky you were with her, otherwise she may not have pulled out of it. We're going to keep her for the next two days to make sure she doesn't suffer another seizure."

Ella left her name and number at the nurse's station and asked if someone could call her the minute Ava wakes up.

"Don't worry, we'll take good care of your friend," a male nurse said.

"Thank you," Ella replied and left in tears. As soon as she got in her car, she texted Grace.

When Ella reached Grace's house, she was glad to see the lights were on. Grace was sitting in the living room with a pot of tea. They hugged each other until their tears subsided. Ella sat next to Grace on the couch. "I'm grateful to both Kayla and her mother," Ella said as she reached for a cup of tea. "I cried when Jill offered to come to Point Judith and run the store. I can concentrate on Ava."

Grace nodded. "You can count on me, too." Grace looked at Ella. "I know, she'll listen to you. Ava always needed you more."

"We're both blessed. Think about it. We have the best friends in the world. From Connecticut to Rhode Island, we have our own village," Ella said and meant it. "Ava loves you very much and she trusts you, but yeah, you're a softy when it comes to discipline and right now, Ava needs to know that I am not playing games. Especially, when it involves alcohol."

They sat in their own silence, sipping their tea, worrying about their friend. "Ava is going to get through this," Ella said and then hugged Grace. "Tell me something good. What have you been up to?"

Grace thought about Dylan and how he made her feel loved. She shrugged her shoulders. As much as she wanted to tell Ella about Dylan, she wasn't sure Ella was ready to hear about Grace finding love when she still wasn't over David. Besides, they had a lot on their plate worrying about Ava. "You know me, day care and selling properties."

"Umm, I have some interesting news to share." Ella smiled like a Cheshire Cat. "Remember the wedding I attended? Well, the best man happens to be a firefighter from Long Island looking to transfer to Stratford. Oh, Grace, he is everything I have ever dreamed of in a man."

"What?" Grace said and tucked her legs under her buttocks. "Why didn't you tell me?" She leaned in and hugged her. "I'm so happy for you. Tell me everything."

"Umm, only after you tell me about Dylan."

Grace laughed. "Well, he's not married," she said simply. "His wife passed away two years ago from cancer."

"Sorry to hear about his wife. Ava said the two of you were at a party, dancing." Then she yawned.

"We better get some rest. I have a feeling we have a lot to do over the next few days," Grace said and got up. She picked up the empty tea pot along with her cup and said, "We'll have plenty of time to talk about the men in our lives once we get our girl back on her feet."

At seven o'clock, the next morning, they were drinking their coffee when Ella's cellphone rang. "Hello."

Grace watched as she nodded several times. When she began to cry, Grace immediately became concerned. The call ended and Ella set her phone down telling Grace. "Ava overdosed on a mix of Fentanyl and heroin."

Grace nearly dropped her coffee cup, Ella collapsed in a nearby chair and began trembling. "What the hell, Grace? Was she trying to kill herself?"

"Oh, my goodness," Grace whispers and then lets out a wordless shriek of disappointment.

Ella cleared her throat before saying, "What time can we drop Hudson off at the day care?"

"Eight. I'll get him ready now," she said and ran into his bedroom.

Grace dropped Hudson off at the day care and said she would be back to get him at six that evening. "He can stay for the after-school activities."

"Great," the teacher said as she took his backpack from Grace. "Are you okay?" she asked in a concerning voice.

"I'm fine, my friend and I have to take care of a few things that's all." Grace turned to leave, but then stopped, turned around, bent down and gave Hudson one more hug goodbye. "I love you so much."

"I love you too, Mommy." Then he waved to Ella. "Bye, Aunt Ella."

Ella blew him a kiss from the car. When Grace got in the driver's seat, she told Ella not to let her forget. "He needs to be picked up by six."

"With all this madness, I'll put him in my calendar as an appointment. Hudson. Six. Got it. I hope Ava's awake when we get there," she said and then told Grace she was going to see if a bed was available at the rehabilitation center. "I'm going to call again and see if they have a bed for her."

"I'm going with you when you take her," Grace said. "Not for her sake, but for yours. You'll need someone to catch you. I know you. It won't be easy leaving Ava in her condition."

10

Ella and Grace arrived at the hospital in time to catch the woman heading for the elevator. "Hey, wait," Ella hollered to her. "Grace, that's the woman who came to visit Ava at the store. She may have been the one who gave her the drugs." Ella ran up to the woman, tugged on her arm and spun her around. "Who are you and how do you know my friend?"

"Fuck off," she said and got in the elevator.

Ella went after her like a bull seeing red. Grace took hold of Ella, pulled her out of the elevator and told her it wasn't the time. "Not now. We need to take care of Ava."

When they walked in the room Ava was sound asleep. Both Grace and Ella checked the entire room for drugs. Grace rolled Ava over on her side to look under her. "In case the bitch put something under her ass."

Ella chuckled. "I'm not playing this game. She's going to rehab."

A nurse came out of the bathroom holding an empty bed pan. "If you're talking about Demarko, I didn't let her in the room. I chased her out." The nurse nodded her head telling Grace and Ella. "Demarko is a known user. I went to high school with her." She held up her fist. "She knows better than to mess with me."

Grace and Ella looked at each other before thanking the nurse. "Should we stay with her to make sure no one gets in her room?" Grace asked.

The nurse shook her head. "No, she's pretty torn up about the whole situation. She had a bad night last night. Vomiting the entire time. I think she's learned her lesson." She set the pan next to Ava's buttocks. "Are one of you Ella?"

Ella raised her hand. "I am."

"She was calling for you all night. She kept saying she was sorry."

After the nurse left, Grace and Ella sat in the two chairs near the window waiting for Ava to wake up. Grace tapped Ella on the hand. "Tell me about your fire fighter."

Ella inhaled, smiled and said, "He's six-two, works out every morning for two hours. He has black hair and eyes so blue... I want to—"

"Swim in them?" Ava said and they both jumped up.

"You scared the crap out of us," Grace said and then hugged her.

Ava looked into Ella's eyes. "I'm sorry."

"I'm glad you're alive, but sorry isn't good enough," Ella said and left the room. Out in the hall she called the rehabilitation center for the third time. "It's Ella, again. I'm sorry, but I need to get my friend—"

"Ella, a bed just became available. You may bring her here tomorrow morning."

Ella took a deep shuddering breath and thanked the woman. Then she went back into the room and told Ava she was going to rehab. "Like it or not, you're going to a rehabilitation center."

Ava started to cry. When Grace went to hug her, Ella pulled her back, stepped in closer to Ava and said, "Save your tears for someone else. This is your mistake and you are going to take responsibility for it. Do you hear me?"

Ava had no tears, only sobs. She was trembling, her face was turning red, but she swallowed her pride and agreed to go. "I'll do whatever you want me to do, please don't take the store from me."

Ella shook her head. Looked at Grace before telling Ava. "You did that to yourself. You lost the right to run the store on your own. When you come home from rehab, you'll stay with me and you'll work in the Connecticut boutique until I can trust you."

Tears streamed down Ava's face. Grace turned her back and moved closer to the window. Outside, the sun shone brilliantly in the clear, blue sky. In Ava's room... darkness prevailed as Ella continued to enforce even more rules Ava had to follow. "You're to have no visitors. Only Grace and me. You'll do everything they ask of you and you will attend every damn meeting, class and therapy session."

Grace rubbed her arms vigorously as she listened to Ella's every word. She agreed with her and she knew Ella was giving Ava some of her tough love. Grace turned to face Ava and Ella. "Ava, I stand by Ella. I think everything she is doing is for the best."

Ella handed Ava the box of tissues and when she did their hands touched. Ella swiped her pointer finger across Ava's wrist. "I believe in you. You can do this."

Ava's bottom lip quivered. "How long do I have to stay there?"

"Six months," Ella replied and then sat back down in the chair.

Grace followed Ella's lead and sat down next to her. "Ella and I will be with you. We'll both take you to the clinic. I'll ask Aunt Emily to watch Hudson."

11

Grace's cell phone rang. She held up one finger for Ella to wait a minute, then she stepped into the bathroom. "Hello."

"Hi, Grace, it's Jamie. The peritoneal equilibration test came back. It passed."

Grace took a deep breath. "That's wonderful. Thank you for calling. I'll let him know right now."

Grace disconnected the call and called David.

He answered on the first ring. "Hey, Grace."

"David, good news the perk test came back. You're all set. You can move forward and start putting in the roads." Grace held the phone away from her ear as David hollered.

"Praise God," he shouted and then told her. "I'm taking you to dinner. Where are you?"

Grace glanced toward the room and noticed Ella was texting someone. "I'm at the hospital with Ella. Ava suffered a relapse. We're taking her to a rehabilitation center in Connecticut tomorrow."

"Grace, please, take care of Ava and give Ella my best."

"I promise and I will," Grace said and ended the call.

Ella left specific instructions at the front desk that Ava was not to have any visitors. Only her and Grace were allowed in her room. Then she asked what time Ava could go home the next day. "I'm taking her directly to High Watch Recovery Center in Kent, Connecticut."

"That's a great rehabilitation center," one nurse said. "They have a five-star drug and alcohol program. She'll be in good hands there." She picked up Ava's chart and said, "I'll work on her discharge papers and have her ready to go by eight tomorrow morning."

Another nurse pointed toward Ava's room. "We'll keep a close on her. I've already put a note in her chart not to allow anyone in her room."

That evening, Ella went with Grace to drop Hudson off at Aunt Emily's house. "I haven't seen her in like forever," Ella said as she got out of Grace's car.

Grace put her hand on Ella's arm. "Wait, Shelby has been taking care of Aunt Emily and she's working with her on her new book release. She may be inside."

Ella took a deep breath. "I'm not worried about Mr. Wayne any longer. In fact, she can have him."

Aunt Emily's new house manager opened the door. "She's been expecting you. She's in the kitchen preparing something for all of you to eat. Hello, Master Hudson."

Grace smiled when Hudson gave her a high-five and then ran to see his Aunt Emily.

Aunt Emily had the table set. She prepared chicken thighs with creamy mustard sauce. "I also made a chocolate buttercream cake for dessert," Aunt Emily said as she hugged Hudson. "We are going to have so much fun." Then she gave Ella a big hug and whispered in her ear. "Ava will be just fine, you'll see."

"Thank you," Ella said and squeezed Aunt Emily's hand.

Immediately after they ate dinner, Grace and Ella said their goodbyes. "We have a lot to do before tomorrow," Grace said and Ella echoed her sentiments.

"I have a ton of paperwork that needs to be filled out before we get there," Ella said and hugged both Hudson and Aunt Emily. "It was so nice seeing you."

"Likewise, and please give Ava my best. Tell her we are all praying for her."

"Thank you," they said in perfect unison.

As soon as they reached Grace's house, Ella phoned the hospital to check on Ava. When she hung the phone up, she told Grace everything they had said. "Ava ate her entire dinner, apparently, she developed an appetite for sugar. She asked for a few more cookies. They said that's a good sign." Ella shrugged her shoulders. "I hope so."

Grace made a pot of tea and set out the two slices of Aunt Emily's chocolate cake for them to eat while filling out all the paperwork. "Done and done," Ella said as she moved the pile of papers to the side and took her last bite. "Thank God you had a printer, I would still be filling in the blanks on my cellphone, never mind I hate Adobe forms."

Grace moved to the floor, stretched out her legs and leaned back resting her head on the sofa. "Tell me about your firefighter."

"He's funny, and he's everything I have ever dreamed of wanting." She sat down next to Grace and clinked her teacup to Grace's. "The first time we were together, he carried me into his bedroom." Ella laughed out loud. "I banged my head on the door jamb, we spun around so fast, my foot knocked over the champagne bucket. Ice went flying on the floor and all over the bed. We laughed so hard that night." She set her teacup down on the coffee table. "Grace, he takes my breath away."

"You slept with him?"

Ella laughed again. "Yeah, if you saw him... you would too." She slapped Grace on the leg. "I'm a big girl, some would say a lady and oh my, was I ready for him. Don't get your feathers in a ruffle, we went out on several dates before I told him, my body was about to explode. I was so hungry for him." She bit her bottom lip. "When he kisses me, I want to—"

"Geez, enough," Grace said and moved her legs up to her chest. "Dylan hasn't even attempted to get that close."

"How long have the two of you been dating?"

"Long enough for him to make his moves," Grace said. "I'm ready to get married and have more children. We get along great; the boys enjoy playing together, but—"

"But what?" Ella asked and a long moment later went by before Grace answered her.

"I don't think he's over his dead wife." She quivered. "He says he's interested in me, but all I get are hello and goodbye kisses. Grace had a look on her face that carried so many emotions.

"Do you dream about him?" Ella asked her.

"Every night, since we met. I'm so ready to be loved and to love someone. I want happiness in my life."

"It will happen. Trust me, when you least expect it, he will be all over you. Just don't bang your head."

They both laughed. Ella held up a finger. "Where do penguins go to watch a movie?"

Grace smiled gingerly and shrugged her shoulders. "Where?"

"To a dive-in." Ella swatted Grace on the leg. "Brody is full of jokes. Every night before we go to sleep, he tells me a new one. He said if we hear a joke before we go to sleep, we'll have beautiful dreams." Ella got up and said, "We have a long drive tomorrow and a very hard day ahead of us. Let's get some sleep."

Grace agreed and she too stood up. "Good night, Ella." Before she turned to go into her bedroom she added, "Here's to penguins and sweet dreams."

"Hey, Grace," Ella called out from the guest room.

"Yeah," Grace replied as she pulled down the bedspread.

"I'm glad you're coming with me tomorrow." Ella inhaled. "It won't be easy leaving her again."

Grace felt tears sting her eyes. She knew it was her fault Ava moved to Point Judith. "I'm sorry I ever left you," she whispered and climbed into the bed.

By the time Grace woke, Ella had coffee brewed, scrambled eggs and toast on the table. "Good morning. Hey, what did the stamp say to the envelope on Valentine's Day?" She said as she poured Grace's coffee.

Grace sat down at the table. Ella kissed her on the top of her head. "I'm stuck on you."

Grace chuckled. "Maybe, I should use that line on Dylan."

Ella looked up at the clock. "It's almost seven-thirty, let's get a move on. I want to be on the road by ten." Then she asked Grace a few questions about Dylan. "How many dates have the two of you been on?"

Grace took her last bite, got up to and cleared the table. She stood at the sink, resting her hands on the counter. "Lunch, dinner, lunch with the boys and dinner at my house or his with the boys."

Ella gave her a seductive smile. "You could always stay home, leave Hudson at Aunt Emily's and invite Dylan for a sleepover."

"No way, am I letting you go through this alone, besides he'd still have Devon with him." Grace batted her eyebrows.

"Maybe, I could ask Aunt Emily to take both boys, she loves Devon and she offered to watch them when I go moonlight fishing for catfish and bullhead next week."

They got into Ella's car. Ella watched as Grace sat motionless. She appeared to be deep in thought. "A penny for your thought?" Ella asked as she started the car.

"I think I'm falling in love with Dylan. Ella, I can't stop thinking about him. I know it's real because I—" Grace looked away.

"What?" Ella said softly as she turned onto the main road. "You can tell me anything. Grace?"

"I don't think about Hudson." She turned to face Ella. "I used to think about him every day. I cried for him for—"

"Too long," Ella said. "I'm sorry. I shouldn't have said that. You cried for Hudson for as long as you needed to cry for any one person. Grace, it's about time you opened your heart again. Maybe, you should tell Dylan how you feel."

"Is that what you did with," Grace looked at her. "I'm sorry, what's his name?"

Ella laughed. "Brody. Quick story before we get to the hospital. I had my hands full at the boutique and he went back to Long Island, so I didn't see him for a few days. I was getting ready for bed and my cellphone chimed. He sent me a video singing, "Wonderful Tonight" in the shower. When the song was over, he said I was all he thought about and he missed me. I cried seeing him naked. I wanted him so bad." Ella smiled, took in a deep breath and said, "The next thing I know, he was standing at my door wearing only his fireman's jacket and boots." Ella pulled up to the hospital, parked the car and told Grace the rest of her story. "Brody was holding me in his arms when I told him that I loved him and wanted to spend the rest of my life with him." She turned to face Grace, touched her cheek and continued. "I took my shot. Either he was going to run or stay. He took my face in his hands and told me he waited his whole life for me. Please don't tell Ava this, but Brody asked me to marry him."

Tears were streaming down Grace's face. Laughingly, she cried, "These are the happiest tears... I have ever cried. I am so happy for you." She chuckled. "I can't believe he sexted you." Grace grabbed a tissue and said, "When? Where?"

"We both like Whittemore in Middlebury; it's the most gorgeous venue in Connecticut." Ella started to cry when Grace held her hands together and prayed.

"Dear Heavenly Father, thank you for sending Ella her one true love."

"Amen," Ella said and opened her car door.

By the time Ella and Grace got to the hospital, Ava was up, dressed and waiting for them in the chair by the window. "I saw you pull into the parking lot. Why were the two of you crying?"

Grace walked up to her and hugged her. Ella patted Ava on the shoulder and told her it had nothing to do with her. "We were crying because we—"

"We're both glad you're alive," Grace said and pointed to the vase of flowers on her nightstand.

"They're from Aunt Emily and David," Ava said. She handed the card to Grace. "Praying for you. Love, Aunt Emily and David."

After they checked Ava out of the hospital, both Grace and Ava fell asleep in the car. Ella turned on the radio and listened to WCTY 97.7. She laughed listening to Scotty McCreedy singing, "Cab In A Solo" thinking of Brody the whole time. Ella wanted to make sure Ava knew she was not backing down; she was determined to see her maid of honor stand by her side on her big day.

Grace woke in a panic. "Oh, my God. I should have

driven my own car. Now you need to drive me all the way back to Point Judith."

"Relax," Ella told her. "Brody said he wants to meet you."

"Who is Brody?" Ava asked as she sat up in the backseat.

"A man I have been seeing," Ella told her.

"The guy you had to dance with at the wedding you went to?" Ava asked and then reached for a bottle of water.

"Yes," Ella replied as she looked in the rearview mirror. "We hit it off so well, we have been seeing each other on a daily basis."

"I'm sorry I took you from him," Ava said and drank her water. When she looked out the window, she asked if they could stop at the next gas station for candy. "Can we get some chocolate at the next gas station, please?"

Ella smiled at her and told her she filled a cooler full of goodies. "I have an entire cooler just for you, my sweet." Then she pulled the car over at the next rest area. "Ahh, I want to stretch my legs." Ella walked to the back of the car, opened the hatch and grabbed the cooler. When she set it on the backseat next to Ava, she said, "I'll have a Payday, please."

Ava opened the cooler and smiled. Tears streamed down her face. "You bought all my favorite candy. I'm sorry, I'm so emotional." She wiped her eyes. "Grace, do you want a water and a Snickers?"

"Sure," Grace said reached back and took the candy bar from Ava.

"Ella, can I get you a water?" Ava asked and then ate two Reese's and a Kit Kat bar.

When they reached the clinic, Ella and Grace had to say goodbye to Ava in the lobby, from there Ava was on her own. "You can do this," Ella whispered and Grace nodded in agreement.

Then Grace shouted, "We love you."

Along with taking Ava's cellphone and all her personal belongings, the woman at the front desk asked if they had Ava's documentation.

"Yes, I do," Ella said and proceeded to hand her the papers.

The woman looked over the application, health insurance information and then slid Ella's check back to her. "You can have this back. Her entire stay has been paid for."

Ella looked at Grace. "You?"

Grace shook her head. "No. I'll bet David paid her bill."

The woman looked down and said she had everything she needed. As soon as Ella and Grace got in the car, they cried. Grace hugged Ella and told her Ava was going to beat her addiction. "You did everything you could. Now, it's up to her. She loves you and she loves working in fashion. The store allows her to share her work with so many people. She'll be okay, you'll see."

Ella wiped her eyes. "I hope you're right." Then she gave Grace a pointed look and dialed David's number. "Hi."

"Hi, back," David said. "How's Ava?"

"That's why I'm calling. David, thank you for paying for her stay at High Watch, but you didn't have to do that. I can afford to—"

"Ella, I didn't. Aunt Emily paid for her favorite fashionista's treatment. Aunt Emily loves all of you. She said you chose one of the finest rehabilitation centers in the country. Ava means a lot to Aunt Emily."

Ella looked over at Grace and said, "It was Aunt Emily. Oh, David. I'll be sure to thank Aunt Emily, myself."

"You got it. We're all rooting for Ava."

"Thank you. Bye. Oh, wait. Grace wants to say something.

Grace started to tell David that she would be home on Sunday, but he said he had to go.

"Grace, I have to go, Shelby is in trouble."

Ella drove to the inn, parked the car and called Brody. "We're here. Okay, sounds good and thank you." She hung the phone up and told Grace, Brody was bringing dinner and he would be there in a half hour. "I can't wait for you to meet him. He's dying to meet my maid of honors."

Ella waited for Grace to respond. "Well, say something," she said and nudged Grace on her shoulder. "Will you be my maid of honor?"

Through happy tears she said, "Yes." And then she hugged Ella. "I would be honored to stand by you."

"Thank you, now get out of the car because I have to use the bathroom." They each grabbed their overnight bags, and a bag full of snacks, wine and beer, thanks to Brody.

When Ella came out of the bathroom, Grace was in the living area pouring two glasses of wine. "A toast to Ava getting the help she needs and to my best friend for finally falling in love."

Ella accepted the glass and tapped her glass to Grace's. "To Ava and to my new man."

They sat on the sofa, sipping their wine and talked about getting Ava on the road to recovery before anything else. "I want both of you standing next to me when I get married. Ava is my priority and Brody knows it." Ella looked at Grace. "What?"

"I just hope she doesn't find a way to get drugs while she's there. I read about a few cases where alcoholics and drug attacks make friends with the staff and get them to buy their—"

Ella shook her head. "Not at High Watch. Trust me, they

run a tight program. Besides, she doesn't have any money or anything else for that matter to offer them."

"It's Ava, she's smart." Grace curled her lip up. "She always gets what she wants and you of all people know it."

"What the hell is that supposed to mean?" Ella set her glass down just as Brody knocked on the door. Ella shook her head at Grace, stood up and kissed Brody hello. "Brody, this is Grace. Grace." Ella held her hand out to Brody. "I'd like you to meet the love of my life."

In a deep, sexy voice, Brody said, "It's nice to finally meet you. Ella has told me so much about you and how proud she is of you."

Grace took one look and knew exactly why Ella fell head over heels in love. Brody had a clean and wholesome look about him. A man you wanted to sit next to at a church function and in the back seat of your momma's station wagon. She extended her hand to him. "It's nice to meet you. Thank you for putting the smile back on her face and for exciting her heart."

Brody gave Ella a hug and when he did, Grace said, "You make a gorgeous couple."

"Thank you," he said with another kiss to Ella's temple. "I love her and I intend on marrying her as soon as we get Ava back on her feet. Right, Babe," Then he set the food on a small table.

"Oh, yeah," Ella said and then asked if everyone was hungry. "Am I the only person starving?"

"That's right," Grace said. "We haven't had anything to eat all day." And then announced, "Oh, wait, she fed us each a candy bar."

Ella smiled and winked at Brody. "Thanks to Brody for filling the cooler." She motioned for them to help themselves. "Grace, more wine? Brody, wine or beer?"

"I'll take a beer, please," he replied as he opened the takeout containers and then said, "I heard you like zuppa di pesce."

Grace smiled knowing Ella requested her favorite dish just for her. "I do," she said and held her glass up for more wine.

Ella refilled both of their glasses before setting three plates, plasticware and paper napkins on the coffee table. "Help yourselves."

Grace noticed Brody lean in for a kiss before taking his first bite. "Thanks for inviting me," he teased.

Grace set her fork down, swallowed the lump in her throat and looked into Ella's eyes. "I'm sorry. I should not have said that to you." Referring to her earlier comment about Ella always giving Ava whatever she wanted.

Ella touched Grace on her shoulder. "It's okay and you're right, I do spoil the people I love."

Brody took a sip of his beer, and then announced he had some good news. "My transfer came in today. I'm officially a Stratford fireman."

Ella leaned over and hugged him. "No more traveling." She clapped her hands and told Grace. "Brody is a top earner, so he had to make sure he was accepted for the position he applied for before he transferred."

"Congratulations, I'm happy for the two of you."

"Thank you," Brody said and asked if he should open another bottle of wine.

Ella put her hand over her glass. "I'm good." She pointed to Grace. "Grace?"

Grace laughed. "No thank you. I'm buzzing from having an empty stomach."

After they ate, they sat in the living area talking about wedding plans and getting Ava back to work. "I'm glad you told Ava she had to work with you before sending her back to Point Judith," Grace said and Brody agreed with her.

"She'll need close supervision for a while," he said. "I hate to say this, but I can't tell you how many times addicts slide back into the same old routine."

"It's the truth," Grace said. "She needs to know that we are watching her every minute and that we care about her."

"There was no way I was going to allow her to run the store on her own, besides with Jill and Kayla running both stores I'll be able to focus on her and our wedding."

Brody kissed Ella on the lips and said, "Grace, Ella tells me you're in real estate. By any chance can you sell my house on Long Island?"

"Of course," she said and pursed her lips. "Do you have a timeline in mind?"

"Immediately," he said. "As soon as you sell it, we're buying a parcel of land and building a big farmhouse."

Ella laughed aloud. "Brody comes from a line of twins." She pointed to him and said, "He wants six, yes, six kids. I told him he had to do it within three pregnancies."

Brody leaned over and hugged Ella. "Whatever you say, you're the person who has to carry them."

Ella kissed him telling him she hoped their children grew up with Grace and Ava's. "I want our children to grow up together."

Grace thought about Ella's idea and for the first time since she left Connecticut, she wished she still lived in Stratford.

"Ladies, can I interest the two of you in a movie and a little popcorn?"

Ella looked at Grace. "When Brody says movie and popcorn he means business." She raised her eyebrows. "He makes the best popcorn."

"I'm game," Grace said. "Can I do anything?"

"Nope, just enjoy your time with Ella. Oh, I'll have Ella text you my address on Long Island."

Brody returned with a big bowl of popcorn sprinkled with Truffle salt. "Let's see, we have Only The Blaze, Burn, and Fire Starter."

Ella laughed. "Welcome to my world."

"I'm kidding," Brody said and turned on Netflix. "I heard you and Ella have been enjoying Virgin River." When he clicked on the network, it went right to the episode they were both watching.

After the movie, Brody announced he was headed back to Ella's house. "I need to get ready for work. I'll see you ladies Sunday night."

Ella walked him out to his truck, kissed him goodbye and thanked him for driving Grace back to Point Judith. "Thank you for everything. I mean it, from the cooler to dinner and for being okay with me staying here for the weekend." She kissed him.

He wrapped his arms around her and said, "I completely understand you wanting to be close by. You're a good person, and that is one of the things I love about you."

She laughed. "Huh, one of? What else do you love about me?"

Brody glance up at the inn, winked and said, "Sext me later, and I'll let you know."

13

D avid raced out of his house and ran down to the beach in time to stop Shelby from getting into a fight with a guy twice her size. "Shelby," David yelled and both Shelby and the man turned to face him. "What is going on?"

The guy threw his hands up in the air and then started to walk away. David reached out and touched his elbow. "Care to explain what just happened?"

"Ask your friend. All I did was pay her a compliment and she slugged me."

David had all he could do not to laugh. Before he turned to face Shelby, he told the guy he should know better than to get that close to her when she was working. "She enjoys what she does. She doesn't like to be disturbed. I'm sure she didn't mean anything." David scratched his neck wondering if Shelby's handprint would vanish from the guy's cheek before night fall. He walked closer to where Shelby was standing and asked her again if she was okay. "Are you sure you're good? What did he say to you that got you so upset?"

Shelby spun around to see the guy walking down the beach. "Say? He put his hand on my ass and said he wanted to take a bite out of it." She started to laugh. "So, I slugged him."

David cleared his throat, shook his head and said, "Good for you, but I have a feeling your handprint isn't going anywhere too soon. Maybe, next time—"

"What? Let him get away with it and thank him?"

"No," David said and raised his hand in the air. "Absolutely not. I just don't want to see you get into a brawl with a man twice your size."

"I can handle myself, David. Trust me. He's not the first asshole to try and put the moves on me." She looked up at the clouds and said she needed to leave. "I better get going. I have the GTO and the top is down."

David looked past the crowd of people and saw the blue vehicle. "That's a nice car." Then his cellphone rang and he told her he would see her another time. "Looks like I need to get going as well." He answered his call. "David Wayne. What? Seriously? I'm on my way."

Shelby bent down and picked up her camera bag. "Is everything okay with Aunt Emily?"

"She's fine. That was one of the housekeepers at the inn. Apparently, I have a manager going rogue." David walked Shelby to her car and continued walking toward the inn. When he walked in everyone was busy. The hostess was on the phone with a future guest, a wait staff person was taking an order and one of the women in housekeeping was pushing a cart with supplies. He asked her where Sue was. "Excuse me, can you tell me where Sue is?"

The woman pointed to the cleaning closet. "She's not happy. Mr. Wayne, please do something."

David nodded. "I'll do my best," he told her and hurried toward the closet. When he walked in, he heard a woman crying. "Hello? Can I come in?"

Sue jumped to her feet. "I'm so sorry. I had to call you. I had no other choice. She is a wretched woman."

David sat down on the bench and patted the seat next to him for her to join him. "Please take a seat and tell me what is wrong." Sue explained how the general manager yelled at her in front of the guests.

"She screamed at me because I left my cart in the hallway." Sue shook her head. "I only left it there for a minute to go in the room and show the woman where the reset button was for the hair dryer. Even the guest told her she shouldn't yell at the help like that."

"How often does she lose her temper?"

"Every day. If she's not yelling at someone, she's scolding one of us for talking to each other." Sue looked at him and asked, "Are we not allowed to talk to each other?"

David coughed into his fist. "I promise you; no one is going to yell at you ever again." He got up and walked back to his house. He went into his closet and grabbed his baseball cap, sunglasses and a pair of old blue jeans. After he changed his clothes, he went back to the inn and sat in the reception area pretending to be reading a newspaper. Not even five minutes later, his general manager walked out of her office and scolded one of the workers for moving a piece of furniture while a guest was trying to read.

"What in the world are you doing? Can't you see he's trying to read the paper? Are you blind?"

David tossed the paper onto the table, jumped up, removed his sunglasses, his hat and told his general manager he wanted to see her in her office. "Now," David said in a stern voice. The woman followed him into the office, walked around the desk and went to sit down until David told her to pack up her belongings. "You're fired. How dare you speak to anyone in that tone. My workers are good people. They do a fantastic job. I have never received one complaint about my staff. I want you out of here within the next five minutes."

"You're firing me?"

David chuckled. "Yes." Then he opened the door and pointed to the exit door. "How dare you make one of my workers cry; you're lucky I don't press charges against you." David stood there with his arms crossed over his chest. When she walked past him, he told her to give him her keys. "You won't be needing these any longer."

"Why are you firing me? Because I instructed an employee to wait until there were no guests in the lobby before he started moving furniture?"

"He was putting the chair back where it belonged. He didn't make a sound." David shook his head at her. "You saw an opportunity and you pounced. That is not how I want my inn or my employees to be treated. That man was doing his job. Do you know how many people would have walked by that chair and said that's not my job?"

"He should have waited," she protested.

"You speak to everyone as if they are beneath you, and that is intolerable." David remembered the day he was there with Shelby. She offered to get him and Shelby coffee and she told Shelby her work should be hanging in the Metropolitan Museum. "You can be saccharine sweet, when you want to be." She was all smiles that day. "When I interviewed you, I told you my employees were to be treated with respect and dignity." He looked away, inhaled and said, "You looked me right in the eye and said you would treat them as if they were your own family." He pointed his finger toward the door. "I want you to leave."

"I'm appalled," she said and walked away.

"I'm sorry you feel that way, but you are not the woman I hired."

David walked around the desk, opened the computer to the calendar and scheduled a meeting with all his department heads. Then he walked through the inn and asked every employee if he or she had any complaints. At first, many of the employees said they were happy and glad they had a job, but after one man told David about an incident he had with the inn's manager, several other employees admitted to being reprimanded by her as well. A woman raised her hand and said, "She yelled at me for carrying an apple through the inn." She shook her head. "She accused me of stealing it from the kitchen. Mr. Wayne, I give you my word, I brought the apple from home."

One of the maintenance men said, "Mr. Wayne, ever since I got sick, she brings me an apple." He chuckled. "She said an apple a day keeps the doctor away." He shrugged his shoulders. "The apple was for me."

David looked at the woman. "I'm sorry you were mistreated. Especially, for doing something nice for someone else." David apologized to the other employees and ensured each person he talked to that he not only dealt with the situation, but from that moment on he wanted them to personally call him. "No matter what, I want you to know you can call me and count on me to handle whatever it is that is upsetting you."

David went back to the office and printed a flyer stating there was a new work environment in place. If anyone needed to talk to him, they were to call him directly. At the bottom of the flyer was his name and phone number. He walked through the inn observing people working, talking, and laughing. Two employees were sharing stories about spending their weekend with their grandchildren when a guest joined in on the conversation. The three men shared photos and laughs. David grinned as he walked past them. "From now on I want to see more laughter and less crying."

14

——————

Monday morning, David stepped outside and looked up at the sky. Not one cloud. The temperature was already near seventy-two and supposed to get as hot as ninety by noon time. It was the most gorgeous day in August and David was interviewing his last candidate for the general manager job. The gentleman said he used to work at an inn in upstate New York. He had over twenty years' experience and seemed to love working as a hospitality manager.

On his way to the inn, David thought about all the fun he had—watching the kitchen staff prepare mouth-watering meals. Receiving high praise from the guests, often asking for the recipe. Seeing the chef high-five her sous chef at the end of every evening and saying how much they looked forward to doing it all over again the next day, made David feel good.

For three weeks straight, David ran the inn and much to his surprise, he enjoyed doing it. He smiled listening to a maintenance man whistle while he worked. He felt a lump in his throat when his cleaning crew presented him with a thank you card along with a basket of apples. He hung the card in the office as a reminder to always pay attention to his staff and to keep an eye on the big picture.

Ten o'clock sharp, Charlie walked into The Lighthouse Inn and asked to speak to Mr. Wayne. "Hi, I have a ten o'clock appointment with Mr. Wayne."

David turned around and shook Charlie's hand. "Please call me David." They walked to the office where David pointed to one of the chairs in front of the desk for Charlie to take a seat and then he sat beside him. "Tell me why you enjoy working in the hospitality business so much."

Charlie looked at David and said, "I started working at Old Drovers Inn when I was a teenager. When the owners parted ways and couldn't settle on who was going to keep the inn, I had to find work elsewhere. It's in my blood— from serving my guests my signature cocktails to ensuring their stay at the inn created everlasting memories to working with the finest people in the world." Charlie offered a satisfied smile. "Every single person who ever worked for me became family. We take care of each other. Each person under my direction knew how to perform the next person's job. We're a team. If one of my maids called in sick, I made the beds. If my chef was sick, we all worked in the kitchen that day." Charlie chuckled. "I had a mainte- nance guy who made the best linguini with white clam sauce." He held up his hand. "A housekeeper who would make you scream for more when she served her appetiz- ers. Her crab cakes with horseradish cream were to die for."

David leaned in, tilted his head to the side and asked. "Why The Lighthouse Inn? New York has plenty of other inns looking for general managers."

Charlie grinned and pointed a finger at David. "You, you

own the place. I would give my right arm to work for a man like you, to learn from you. You're a legend."

"I'm flattered," David said with a chuckle.

"Mr. Wayne, you are who you are because you trusted your gut. You didn't wait for an opportunity to come your way; you paved the road yourself." Charlie laughed aloud. "And if I may say so myself, you used dough instead of asphalt. When I saw you had an opening on estates dot com, I immediately applied. It would be an honor to work for you. I give you my word, I will not let you down." Charlie took a deep breath. "I know the hours it takes to run an inn—"

David held up a hand. "I hired a woman who ensured me she too knew what it takes." He shook his head. "More than an inn, we have human beings working for us. People who give their all to this inn, and they deserve to be treated with respect and dignity." He stood up. "Take a walk with me. I'd like to introduce you to a few of the workers."

Charlie followed David into the kitchen where he introduced him to his chef. She nodded at Charlie and gave David a thumbs up before setting her wooden spoon down on the counter.

Charlie extended his hand out to her and said he was delighted to meet her and he hoped to be working with her one day. Then David and Charlie entered the laundry room and met a few of the women who clean and do the inn's laundry. Charlie brought his hands together in a prayer like position and said, "You are the backbone of the inn. Thank you for your service and dedication."

David remained apprehensive. He needed to see Charlie interact with the employees when he wasn't around. David thought about the dining rooms' security camera. "Charlie let's go into the dining room next. David introduced Charlie to two of the servers and then he told Charlie he would be right back. "Excuse me for a moment, I need to check on something." David made his way to the office and watched as Charlie greeted guests, poured water and smiled warmly at each of the servers. When he offered a thumbs up to one of them, David was convinced to give him a shot.

David liked the idea of Charlie being in his late fifties, single and willing to transfer to Point Judith on quick notice. When he walked back to the dining room, he could hear Charlie telling two of the servers why he applied for the general manager's position. "I like working with people. I believe in good karma."

"Charlie," David called out and motioned for him to follow him out to the lobby. "I'm sure you know everything there is to know about the inn, but I want you to know in addition to our guests, my staff is just as important to me."

"One hundred percent," Charlie said. "If you would like I can give you a few more personal references. In fact, I can give you one from everyone I ever worked with."

"That won't be necessary. Can I ask you a question?"

"Anything," Charlie replied.

"Do you have a place to stay in Point Judith?"

"I didn't think that far in advance. But I'm sure I could find an apartment if I had to."

David held out his right hand as he welcomed Charlie to the inn. "I'd like to offer you the job and let you know you can stay in one of the rooms until you find a place to live."

Charlie went to hug David but instead put his other hand on David's shoulder. "I promise you I will be the best manager you have ever seen. Thank you, Mr. Wayne."

"Please call me David. Shall we go into the office and discuss your salary and start date?"

Charlie followed David into the office and started work the next day.

15

G race was on the phone with Ella when Hudson asked her if he could have a sleep over. "Mommy, please?"

Grace put her hand on his shoulder and told him she was on the phone with Aunt Ella and they would talk about it later. "Hudson, eat your breakfast." She held up her cellphone. "I'm talking to Aunt Ella about visiting Aunt Ava."

"Sorry." Hudson picked up his fork and began eating his waffles as he listened to Grace talk about driving to Connecticut to see Ava.

"I'll see if Aunt Emily can watch Hudson."

"I'll booked a room at The Litchfield Inn again. I like the fact that it's only a half-hour from the center."

"I do too and I loved the country charm vibe, it felt like we were staying in the woods," Grace said and then told Ella she needed to get going. "I have to take Hudson to day care."

"Bye, Grace. Hugs to Hudson. I'll see you on Friday."

Ella hung the phone up and called Brody. "Hi, handsome. I wanted to let you know that Grace said she would go see Ava with me this weekend, so the house is all yours."

"We'll try not to destroy the place too much," Brody said. "I can't wait to see their faces when I tell them I am getting married."

"As soon as I get home tonight we'll run over to Whole Foods and buy enough beer and snacks to last the entire weekend. Did you make reservations at the Sitting Duck Tavern for Saturday night?"

"Yes, and I thought maybe you and I would go out tonight and celebrate at the Riverview Bistro."

"Sound great. I love you. See you tonight."

"I love you, too," he said and then added, "I'm excited about our future."

Ella allowed a warm smile and her heart to rise thinking about marrying Brody.

After Grace dropped Hudson off at day care, she went straight to David's beach house, knocked on the door and then opened it. "Hello. David? Where are you?" She stepped inside, closed the door and walked through the kitchen. When she reached the living area, she saw him sitting on the back deck, talking on his cellphone. She approached him from behind, gently touched his shoulder and gave him a wave of hello before sitting down next to him. She listened as he told Aunt Emily about hiring a new person to run The Lighthouse Inn.

"You'll like him. Yes, I explained to him how important my staff is to me. Okay, I need to go. Grace just got here and I'm hoping she has good news for me. Love you too, I'll call you tonight with all the details." David ended the call and took a deep breath before asking. "Is Ava, okay?"

"She is on the road to recovery and she is doing well. She passed all her courses and are you ready for this? She doesn't know it yet, but she sold her bathing suit and surf line to Bali for three million dollars."

"What? What do you mean she doesn't know it yet?"

"Ava pitched her line to Bali about a year ago and apparently, they loved it so much they made an offer Ella couldn't refuse. She's not telling Ava until she comes home in January. Ava's counselor said Ava needs to focus on her sobriety and nothing else."

"But wouldn't that give her something to look forward to?"

"Her health is the most important thing right now and she's to have no other distractions. Ella doesn't even want her thinking about the store right now. She wants Ava to concentrate on getting her mind in the right place." Grace offered a wry grin. "I agree with everything Ella says and is doing."

"You're both right," he said and stood up. "Are we still going out to lunch?"

"Yes," she said and tapped him on his head. "You owe me."

To celebrate buying the land, David and Grace enjoyed lunch at Matunuck Oyster Bar in Wakefield. They shared a platter of oysters talking about the parcel and how perfect it was for his community. "The land is perfect," David said. "Flat and open. I don't have to do a lot of clearing and the houses can be delivered as soon as the main road is in."

"I told you it was fate when the first lot sold." Grace's green goddess arrived. "I love sushi. I swear I would eat it every day if I could." She pointed to David's jumbo shrimp and said, "I'll share mine if you—"

He popped one in her mouth. "Delicious, right?"

Grace smiled as she chewed and swallowed. "So good." Then she pointed toward the water. "Is that Shelby?"

Shelby was taking photos of a group of women kayaking on paddle boards. David couldn't take his eyes off them.

"She does the most amazing work. Every shot is perfected. The way she uses the sun, it's like she owns it or talks to the damn thing."

Grace laughed. "I'll bet she can lasso your heart in just as fast if you ever open it."

David focused on his shrimp. Offering the last one to Grace. "How many times do I have to tell you, she's a very nice woman, but a little too young for my blood. I respect her for her ability to take a great photo and that is it."

Shelby caught then looking at her and waved in their direction. When they finished their lunch, David and Grace took off their shoes and walked down to the beach. "Hey," Shelby said.

"Hi," Grace and David replied. Grace pointed out toward the water. "You are everywhere."

"I go where I am needed," Shelby said as she packed up her cameras. "What are the two of you doing?"

"We were celebrating," David replied.

"Gotcha, hey how is Ava doing?" Shelby asked and then shook her head. "I was sick when I heard what happened."

"She's getting much better," Grace said. "Ella and I are going to see her this weekend. I'll let her know you were asking for her."

"Do you think I could go and see her?" Shelby asked as she tossed her camera bag over her shoulder.

"I don't see why not. Let me check with Ella and get back to you." Grace said as she began to walk down the beach toward David's Tahoe. "I promised my boyfriend I would pick the boys up from day care this afternoon."

"Boyfriend?" Shelby asked and pointed to David. "I thought—"

"Umm, yeah. No, we're just friends. Right David?"

"Right," David said and asked Shelby what car she was driving. "Shelby did you bring the Jeep or the GTO?"

Shelby offered him a Cheshire smile. "The GTO."

"Grace, you have got to see this car. It purrs going down the road." David walked around the restaurant and pointed to the blue vehicle. "Gorgeous, right?"

"Wow, I had no idea that car belonged to you. Dylan and I were at The Sweet Spot with the boys the other night when it went by and Dylan almost fell over trying to see it." Grace smiled at David and asked Shelby, "Can you drop me off at David's?"

Shelby laughed. "Sure, let's go. David, it was nice seeing you again." Both Grace and Shelby waved goodbye.

David waved them off and hollered, "Keep it on all fours."

Of course, Shelby had to leave a burn mark in the road. As soon as Shelby got onto Ocean Road, Grace asked her if she would ever consider going out with David.

Shelby blew out a long breath. "Grace, I'd rather go out with Ava."

"Oh," Grace said and turned to look out her window.

"Does that upset you?"

"Hell no," Grace said. "Ava is a grown woman; she can go out with whomever she wants." Grace turned to face Shelby. "Have the two of you ever—"

Shelby made the turn onto Sand Hill Cove when she said, "Kiss? No. We shared a few laughs once and I thought she was just as interested in me as I was in her."

"I was going to ask if the two of ever talked or went out on a date."

"No, we just hung out at the beach one day, but she wrote me a letter and asked me to stop by and see her when she got home."

Shelby pulled up to David's. Grace thanked her for the most enjoyable ride she had ever experienced. "That was a lot of fun. I can't wait to tell Dylan; I rode in his favorite car." Grace got out, closed the door, leaned in and said, "You should definitely go see Ava. It would make me and Ella very happy if Ava were with a woman like you. You are good for her soul." Grace tapped on the door. "We're all blessed to have you in our lives." She smiled. "I wish the both of you so much happiness."

By the time David got home, Grace's car was gone.

Grace sat outside the day care waiting for the boys to come out. She couldn't wait; she had to call Ella. "You are never going to believe what just happened. Shelby asked me if she could go see Ava and—"

Ella cleared her throat. "Is in love with Ava? I know. Ava told me they talked one night and Ava wrote to her. Ava said she had no idea she would be interested in a woman until Shelby. Ava's therapist told Ava maybe that's why she never fully committed to any man."

"Well, I guess I'm last to know again," Grace said. "I'm happy for them. Hey, Shelby asked if she could go up and see Ava, what do you think?"

"I'm not Ava's mother for goodness's sake. From what I hear, Shelby is good clean fun. Why not?"

"I agree. Hey, the boys are coming out. I'll see you tomorrow evening. Love you, bye."

Ella said bye to an empty phone line.

Grace drove over to Dylan's with the boys laughing and giggling in the backseat the entire time. "I wonder what Daddy cooked for dinner?" Devon said as he got out of the car.

"Mommy did Daddy cook for us too?" Hudson asked and Grace almost slammed her fingers in the car door.

She rubbed her fingers making sure they were oaky. "Yes, Hudson we are staying for dinner."

Hudson clapped his hands and ran to the front door with Devon by his side.

Dylan kissed Grace and told the boys to wash their hands. "Hurry up, dinner is on the table."

The entire time they were eating, Grace thought about Hudson referring to Dylan as his dad. That bothered her and she immediately thought she was spending too much time with him. They hadn't even slept together and yet her son was starting to see them as a family.

Dylan and Grace were washing the dishes when Dylan banged his hip into hers. "You're very quiet tonight. Is everything okay?"

Grace dried her hands off and told him, "I just have a lot on my mind." She began putting the dishes away when she said, "I'm still worried about Ava, something Ella said the other day bothered me, but otherwise, I am—.

He kissed her. "I understand."

They heard the boys playing in the living room. Devon was calling for Hudson to come out from under the coffee table. "I found you. You can come out now."

Grace went into the living room and told Hudson it was time to go home. "Come on young man, we have to get going."

"Mommy, can I stay overnight?" Hudson looked at Dylan. "Please?"

Dylan smiled at him and put his hand on Devon's head. "We would love it. Right Devon?"

"Sorry, we already made plans for you to stay at Aunt Emily's this weekend. Maybe next time."

"Okay, Mommy. Bye, Devon."

"Hudson, what do you say to Dylan?"

Hudson hugged his leg and said, "Thank you for dinner."

Dylan kissed Grace goodbye and told her to say hi to Ella and Ava. "I'll see you next week. We'll take the boys out for dinner at Iggy's Doughboys."

"Sounds like fun," she replied and reached for Hudson's hand.

After she got home, tucked Hudson into his bed she called Aunt Emily and asked if she was available to watch Hudson. Then she checked her emails. She was surprised to see she had an email from Steve. "Hi, Grace. I hope you are doing well. We still love the house and every night we thank our lucky stars for you. Thanks again for selling me the house. Funny coincidence, my son is in Jimmy's son's class. He says he misses you and your friends. If you're ever in Connecticut I know he would love to see you and so would I. Okay, take care. Steve.

"Huh, maybe?" She closed her laptop, turned off the light and tried to go to sleep. I haven't seen Jimmy in five years. I suppose I could stop in and say hi. Maybe, I could even swing by and see if Steve did anything new to the house. Bad idea. "Go to sleep, Grace."

Grace was awake for two hours, remembering all the fun she had with Ella and Ava every time they went to see Jimmy at the Stonebridge Restaurant. Jimmy was a good bartender and an even better friend. They never had to ask for their drinks, Jimmy knew exactly what they wanted and how they liked it. He took good care of the women. Watched over them and always made sure they got home safe.

She thought about the first time she met Steve. He was selling his home and she was the listing agent. He took her breath away. He was gorgeous, sexy and yes a bit mysterious looking. "Okay, so he had a gun lying across his lap." Grace didn't care about the shotgun as much as she did the look in his eyes. He appeared lost, lonely and in need of a friend. She was grateful he called her that night to apologize and explain himself. She still had the email from Steve apologizing again for his behavior. The gun belonged to his ex-wife's father. The old gun was for display purposes only. Still, it was uncalled for, he wrote.

During the past four years, Steve and Grace have exchanged emails, keeping each other up to date about their own children and Steve's love for the house. Grace found herself rereading his last email. His words melted her heart especially when he said he would love to have more children.

16

Aunt Emily was excited about the release of her next book. This cookbook featured more recipes, pictures and photos of her lifestyle. Her publisher wanted her fans to get a closer look into the life of their famous chef.

She was sitting on the back deck looking out at the ocean when it occurred to her that David hadn't been formally introduced to Judith Ann. She went inside and called her publicist. "Would you arrange a meeting with the writer, Judith Ann and myself here at my home?"

"I can do that. In fact, I am having lunch with everyone from Penguin next week."

"Great, whatever time works for her. She's right here in Rhode Island, so it shouldn't be too much of a bother for her."

After Emily hung up the phone and called David to see if he would be available. "David, by any chance do you have time for lunch in the next few days?"

"For you, anything. Let me know what day and I will be there."

"Great," she said and smiled to herself.

"I'm glad you called. I have good news. Grace got them to accept my offer, I'm closing on the property in September."

"Oh, David. That is wonderful news. Sounds like we'll both have something to celebrate."

"Yes, your cookbook and my new development."

"If I can be of any assistance, please let me know," she said and ended the call.

Before David could hang up the phone, he heard a knock on the door. He kissed Grace on the cheek and said, "Come on in, I just told Aunt Emily about our deal."

Grace stood there for a moment, smiled up at him and said, "I just got off the phone with Guido's they're a small franchise that offers superior quality goods. They would like to be one of your retailers."

David picked her up and swung her around, then he kissed her on the forehead. "I'm so excited to see this project come to life. Did they mention how many square feet?"

"Slow down, David. I know you're excited but one step at a time." She followed David inside.

They sat in the living room. "This calls for a toast," David said and went out to the kitchen. When he returned, Grace had tears in her eyes. She accepted the glass and smiled up at him. "They better be happy tears," he said.

"They are," she replied and tapped her glass to his. After nearly emptying her glass, she laughed out loud and said, "I had a dream." She wiped her eyes with a tissue. "Because of you, Narragansett no longer had any homeless people." She openly cried. "I'm so glad our paths crossed."

"Me too," he said as he touched her cheek telling her, "You are the sister I never knew I needed. Thank you for breaking into my house."

They both laughed remembering the time she booked his beach house for the summer from a man who had no right renting it out. A long minute went by, Grace studied David's expression before she asked him, "What's wrong?"

"Nothing."

She tapped his hand and said, "I know that look. Something is bothering you."

David made a gesture as if to say it was not important but then said, "I have to make sure they are protected from the wolves after I am gone."

"First of all, you're not going anywhere for a long time to come." Then she looked into his eyes. "Maybe you should ask for help. Ask big corporations to donate enough money to secure the future of the community." She looked at him knowing he hated to ask anyone for anything. "It's okay to ask for help. Think about it. I'm going for a walk down the beach, care to join me?"

"No thank you, I think I'll start working on my design. You got me excited talking about the grocery store." David hugged her and said, "Enjoy your walk."

"One more thing." She rubbed her face. "Guess what I found out? Shelby has a crush on Ava."

"And you wanted me to go with her," he said and chuckled. "Go for your walk."

Up ahead, Grace saw Red carrying a little girl out of the water. A woman was screaming. Grace yelled as she ran to them. "What happened?"

Red set the little girl down on the beach and began CPR. First, he tilted her head back, lifted her chin, and began giving her rescue breaths, then he gave her chest compressions. When he rolled her onto her side, the little girl spat out water and cried. Red took a deep breath. "There you are." He looked up at the girl's mother. "She's okay." He stood up and told Grace the woman was pointing toward the water. "She kept yelling my baby, I had no idea what she was screaming about until I saw the child floating face down in the water."

Grace sucked in a breath, turned around and smiled at the mother holding her child. Then she turned to face Red. "You're a hero."

"Yes," the woman said and thanked him. She hugged him. "Thank you so much." She looked at Grace. "I have no business being here." She shook her head. "I don't know how to swim."

Red nodded his head and began walking away. Grace followed him. "Are you okay? That was—"

"Nothing," Red replied.

Grace laced her arm through his. She kissed him on the cheek. "You're so damn modest. Then her cellphone rang.

"I'll be going now." Red waved goodbye as Grace answered her call.

"Hello." Grace listened as Ella told her about wanting to leave by noon on Friday. "Sounds good. I'll be at your house by eleven." Standing at the water's edge, Grace did a happy dance. She kicked up water, twirled around until she fell in the water. She sat there for a long time, brought her knees up to her chest and hugged them, wondering how and what she had to do to reach Red. It bothered her that he was unwilling and unable to make a connection with her. "You're so deep and so damn introverted," she called out to him.

17

D avid met with his lawyer, Allan and the engineer. His lawyer assured him the planning board and the zoning board were on board with the new subdivision. "The state of Rhode Island would like to offer you an emergency solutions grant in the amount of half a million dollars." Allan handed David a folder. "The grants don't stop there. The CoC program and HUD just announced they also have available over two-point-eight billion in annual funding."

"That's great, but I don't require funding, I need—"

"Hang on, David. Who is going to finance the project after the construction is completed? It's not like anyone will be paying rent."

David nodded. "I'll set up a trust fund."

"Okay, but why use all your money? Take some of the grant money and put that into the trust for future taxes." Allan stood up and grabbed a book down off the shelf. "Read this." He handed the book to David.

David accepted the book and thanked them both for

their help. "I'm on my way to meet with John to see if his crew will be available. I'd like to start as soon as possible."

Allan shook David's hand. "I'll do all I can to get this closed on time."

David was sitting in his Tahoe when his cellphone rang. He tossed the book on the passenger seat and answered the call. "Hello."

"Hey, I'm stuck in traffic," John said. "You can definitely count on us."

"Great," David replied. "We should be able to start by the first of October." David set his cellphone down and picked up the book "Government Grants for Dummies" and laughed. "Looks like I have some homework to do this weekend."

He got out of the vehicle and had to blink against the rain and sand blowing in his direction. The wind buffered the shore, and the gray sky seemed to have dropped to the ocean, making every wave higher than the one before. He looked out hoping the men and women surfing stayed safe and out of harm's way. A moment later, three more people ran toward the water. Surfboards tucked under their arms, smiles so broad one could see their tonsils. He went into the house and ordered dinner for himself. Afterwards, he read the entire book, made a few notes and climbed into bed.

Six a.m., he laced up his jogging sneakers and headed down the beach. Dr. Ferris had every light on and three houses down from him the writer had her lights on too. He ran three miles along the ocean, turned back around and was headed home when he saw Jude waving to him.

"I thought that was you," she said. "I thought I was the only person foolish enough to be awake this early in the morning. Care for a cup of coffee?" She was wearing jeans, a crisp white tee shirt and had on a pair of loafers as if she was ready to go somewhere. Her long dark hair was tied up in a ponytail and David thought she looked beautiful.

"I would love a cup," he replied and walked a little closer to her. "Should I run home and shower first?"

She laughed. "It's just a cup of coffee." She motioned for him to follow her. "You're fine."

He followed her inside. The house was different from the last time he was in it. "Everything is brand new," he said as he accepted his cup.

Jude looked around. "I was surprised when I saw how beautiful everything was. I searched for days looking for a place to rent and then one day this place popped up. The realtor said the daughter remodeled the place and was going to sell it but decided to hold onto it for a while. Someone was looking out for me."

David drank his coffee and he too looked around noticing the new kitchen cabinets, wallpaper and tile flooring. "The floors used to be all hardwood."

"I can't imagine what years of sand would do to a hardwood floor."

"I'm blessed to have a housekeeper, but on occasion I have been known to use a broom. If you're still looking for someone to show you around, I'd be glad to oblige."

"I would appreciate that so much. I'm writing a new series about three couples living in a beach community. So, I'm interested in the lifestyle, places and events that take place."

"Then you chose the right place, because Point Judith has everything you're looking for. I can show you around today if you'd like."

"Umm, sure if you have the time," Jude said and sipped

her coffee. "Can I interest you in a second cup? I always make a full pot."

David lifted his cup up. "Are you always up at this hour?"

She poured him another cup and said, "Like clockwork, four a.m. so I can watch the sun rise." She laughed aloud. "It's when my creative juices start to flow. Sometimes, my characters wake me up in the middle of the night, forcing me to write." She shrugged her shoulders. "What can I say? I love what I do."

"I'm an early riser myself."

"I can see that." She laughed. "The first day I noticed you, I thought someone was chasing you, but then I noticed you running at the exact same time every day. I didn't know it was you until Dr. Ferris told me." She leaned back in her chair, looked over her shoulder and asked, "Would you like breakfast? I make the best blueberry pancakes."

"No, thank you," he replied and set his coffee cup down on the table. Anything you would like to see first?"

"No, umm yes. Everything." She laughed. "Whatever Point Judith has to offer."

David stood up. "I know exactly where we should start. Let me run home, take a shower and I'll pick you up at nine." David turned to say, "Bring a bathing suit."

Jude shook her head. "I'm sorry to say I don't know how to swim."

David was not one to judge. Anyone else would have asked her why she rented a house on the beach, if she didn't know how to swim. "Don't worry, I have life jackets. I'll teach you. If you would like—"

"I would love to learn how to swim." She tilted her head to the side. "You are amazing. Tour guide, swimming instructor. Is there anything else I should know about you?"

David chuckled. "I was a lifeguard at the old Dutch Inn,

so you're safe with me and if you're going to live in Narragansett for a whole year, you should know how to at least keep yourself afloat." He pointed toward the ocean. "Besides, how can you not go in the water?"

Jude offered him a crimson smile as she waved goodbye.

"I'll see you in a little while," he said and walked toward the door.

"David," she called out to him. "Thank you." She smiled warmly. "For offering to show me around and to teach me how to swim. That's very kind of you."

David returned at a quarter after nine. He knocked on the door and held up a gift bag. "Ava's personal design."

"Speaking of Ava, how is she?" Jude asked and then graciously accepted the bag. "If you don't mind me asking." She raised her eyebrows. "I think I missed a few chapters."

"We all did," David replied. "She's in rehab. I had no idea she had a problem until the day of Dr. Ferris's party."

Jude looked in the bag and smiled. "It's beautiful. Thank you."

David held the door open for her. "Are you ready?"

She nodded and followed him down the beach. The tall, sparse grass weaved through the wild roses as a salty breeze swept over them, cooling their skin. "I have a confession to make. This is my first stroll along the water," she said.

He glanced over at her. She wore little to no make-up. He offered her a rueful grin. "Salty Brine Beach is a tiny beach, barely a hundred yards long, the gentle surf is set close to the busy Galilee docks and several seafood restaurants. There's a three-mile sea wall that protects the surf. That's why you see a lot of children. The wall keeps them safe from high tides. So, trust me, your guiding angel sent you to the right beach."

She laughed. "I like that idea and yes, I'm grateful for the wall. I'm not big on children," she said with honesty in her voice. "I suppose it's because I love my job so much." She waited for him to respond, but when he did not, she said, "In the afternoons when I am creating my social media posts or doing research, I enjoy watching the fishing boats, pleasure boats and seeing the ferry going by, until the kids start their shenanigans."

David pointed toward the water. "Have you ever been on a cruise ship or a private yacht?"

She shook her head. "Sorry. I'm a bore, right?" She laughed aloud. "I never had the time or desire. Besides, I figured everyone would laugh at me for wearing a life vest the entire time."

David stopped walking for a second. "You don't have to be embarrassed about protecting yourself from danger. "I have an idea," he said and turned back around. As they walked, he told her about all the attractions Salty Brine Beach had to offer. "Besides swimming, there's picnicking, saltwater fishing, you'll want to watch the volleyball tournament. Both men and women come from all over the world to play in the tournament." David pointed to his Tahoe. "It's time you started having a little more fun in life." As soon as David got in, he called Bill. "Bill, can you be ready in a half hour?"

Bill told him he was ready. "Perfect timing, I just stocked the galley," he replied.

David sent Bill a quick text letting him know it was Jude's first time on a yacht and she did not know how to swim. When David pulled up to the Bill Pay, Jude's eyes opened wide. "I read about your yacht. Wow, it's even more beautiful up close." She blushed adding, "I Googled you the day you helped Ava. Very impressive."

Bill held his hand out to her as he welcomed them

aboard. Cory James handed Jude a life vest. He too had one on. When he winked at David, David mouthed the words, "Thank you."

Jude turned to David and said, "I feel safe with you." Then she handed the vest back to Cory James.

18

It had been six weeks since Grace and Ella saw Ava. They were so excited to go see her. As soon as Grace dropped Hudson off at Aunt Emily's house, she called Ella to say she was on her way. "I'll be there by ten. I'm excited too," she said and ended the call. She turned the radio on and listened to KC101, a popular station in Connecticut. She thought about stopping by and visiting Jimmy at the bar on her way home. She wondered how big his children were getting. They never got to meet his little girl. Then a warm smile appeared as she thought about her and Steve texting back and forth. Nothing serious, mostly about their children and their first encounter. Steve made Grace feel good inside. There was something about him that made her want more of him.

Friday traffic was impossible. It didn't matter what direction you were driving. "Oh, my goodness, let's go," she hollered at the car in front of her. She turned off I-95 onto South Avenue and pulled into the first gas station she saw. After using the bathroom, she texted Ella. "I'll be there in fifteen minutes."

"Yay, I'm so excited to see you and to go see our girl. Brody filled my car with gas and packed us a great cooler for the ride."

Grace pulled into Ella's driveway and saw a group of men getting out of a pickup truck. Ella waved to her as she parked the car on the street in front of the house. When she got out, Brody assisted her with her bags. "It's nice to see you again and thanks for listing the house. I heard you showed it a few times," he said.

Grace hugged Brody and told him she may have an offer on the place. "I ordered a home inspection, if everything goes the way I think it will, you should be able to close sometime in October."

Brody waved for Ella to come closer. "Grace may have an offer on my house."

"I told you she was the best realtor for the job." Ella hugged Grace and asked Brody to introduce her to his friends.

Fifteen minutes later, Grace and Ella were on their way to see Ava. "I couldn't sleep last night, I was so excited," Ella said as she turned onto CT-25 toward Kent.

"I hope she's doing as well as they say." Grace looked at Ella. "Ava can be very persuasive when she wants to be."

"She can," Ella replied adding, "But I think she's happy now. Her letters seem upbeat." Ella held out her hand and started to say something but stopped herself.

"What?" Grace asked, looking at Ella to finish her thought.

"Ava is in her glory. She met a lot of nice people. A lot of the women wear her designs and—"

"What, for heaven's sake. What is going on?" Grace was getting angry at Ella. "Please don't make me feel like the third wheel again."

"What?" Ella said as she turned onto Hanover Road. "We never made you feel like—"

"You have," Grace said adding, "And you know it. Do I have to remind you about the incident in the tenth grade when you and Ava had a sleep over and never bothered to ask me if I wanted to join, or how about the time the two of you decided to go see my favorite movie without me?" Grace stared out the window before saying, "I've always felt like the stepsister."

Ella pulled the car over to the side of the road. "I'm sorry we made you feel that way. Grace, you're my best friend. If I ever needed someone in my life... it's you. I do what I can for Ava because she requires more of my attention, but it's always been you."

Grace had tears in her eyes. Laughingly she cried, "And you're my best friend."

Ella put the car in drive, turned toward Grace and asked, "I don't' remember going to the movies without you." She slapped Grace on the leg. "Wait a minute. You said you couldn't go."

"Yeah, so. You should have waited," she teased. "Thank God, we're here. I need to pee."

Up ahead Ella could see the sign for the inn. "Let's have a glass of wine before we head over to the center."

"No," Grace replied. "Ava will smell it on our breaths. We'll have plenty of time to drink when we get back. I want to go see her as soon as we can."

They checked in, brought their bags and carried the cooler inside. As soon as they reached the rehabilitation center, they both became emotional. "She needed to miss us," Ella said.

"I hope she missed us as much as we did her," Grace said and popped a breath mint in her mouth. "Want one?"

Ella took the mint and said, "Let's go out to dinner tonight. I have so much I want to talk to you about."

"The wedding, I hope."

They parked the car and started walking toward the office when they heard Ava calling out their names. "Ella. Grace."

Ava was a picture of pure beauty. She was radiant. She had gained a few pounds and her hair was much longer. They both held their arms out to her. The three women cried, holding each other as other visitors walked by.

Grace pointed to a bench under a shade tree. "Let's sit over there. Ava, you look remarkably well. I'm so proud of you."

"You look happy. Are you happy, Ava?" Ella asked as she sat down on the bench.

Ava sat in the middle. "I have a new shrink," she said, looking pensively at the front door.

"Oh," Ella said quietly.

"Do you like your new therapist?" Grace asked as she stroked Ava's hair.

"I do," Ava said. "She's kind and considerate. She doesn't pressure me to always have the right answers. Like when she asked me what I treasured the most in my life."

Ella put her arm around her and squeezed her shoulder. "Are you allowed to share with us?"

Ava held her hands up to her face, then pulled them away and said, "I treasure our friendship the most."

"That's nice," Grace said adding, "we feel the same way about you, right Ella?"

Ella nodded in agreement and said, "In your last letter you said you made a few new friends."

"Yes," Ava said and turned to face Ella. "No, they are not recovering alcoholics or drug addicts. They're employees.

The secretary wears my pants to work every day and my therapist said she loves my entire line of clothing." Ava turned to face Grace. "Guess what?"

"What, sweetheart?" Grace said and smiled.

"I met a celebrity. He's friends with the previous founder's son. You would never know he was famous, he's so down to earth and friendly."

"Are you allowed to mingle with the guests?" Ella asked hoping she wasn't about to get herself into trouble.

"He's on the approved visitors list," Ava said. "You can check."

"Ava, I'm not your mother. I just want to make sure you're not getting yourself into any trouble."

"You sound like my mother," Ava said and stood up. "I'm sorry. I know you care about me and yes you have a right to be, but sometimes—"

"I can be a bitch," Ella said and meant it. "You're right. I do mother you." She stood up and pointed to Grace. "Just ask Grace, she's been telling me that forever." Ella hugged Ava. "I'm happy you met someone. Does he live in California?"

"No, he lives right here in Kent."

"Oh," Ella said and turned toward Grace. "Do we get to meet him?"

"Not until graduation. Apparently, he comes every year and makes a speech. Oh, I invited Shelby, Aunt Emily and David," Ava said.

"Sounds nice," Ella said and started to walk toward the building. "Ava, did anyone tell you who paid for your stay here at High Watch?"

"You did, right?" Ava said and kicked a pebble off the sidewalk.

Ella shook her head. "Aunt Emily paid for your entire stay before we even arrived."

Ella and Grace smiled at each other, but when Ava started to cry, they both reached out and hugged her. "It's okay. Aunt Emily loves you so much," Ella said.

"Ava," Grace said and stood back. "You are very special to a lot of people. You're not alone. We." Grace moved her hand in a circle. "We have an entire village of good people who love us and care deeply for us."

"I have a confession to make," Ava said as she wiped away her tears. "Before coming here, I had days when I didn't want to live. Now, I want to live every day to my maximum potential." She held her hands up in the air. "I want to design my clothes, I want to have babies, I want—"

She smiled warmly at them. "I want us to be like we used to be... happy, together and I want to sit on the floor and drink tea, talk about our lives and laugh again."

They heard the first bell letting them know their time was almost up. "I'm okay," Ava said. "You can go. I'll be here waiting for you." She kissed their cheeks and said, "I need to go."

"We'll see you tomorrow," Ella said and waved goodbye as she put her other arm around Grace.

Grace hollered out to her. "Wait, we have a present for you." Grace handed Ava a friendship bracelet.

Ava smiled at it and laughed. "It's adorable, but I can't take it. Gifts aren't allowed." She ran toward the door. "But I love it and I love you guys so much."

They were on their way to dinner when they both looked at each other. "We never asked her what the actor's name was," Grace said.

"Trust me, I will investigate." Ella said as she pulled into the restaurant.

Ella and Grace went to the Fife 'n Drum for dinner. When asked if they wanted a cocktail in perfect unison they asked for a glass of water with lemon. They both had the French onion soup for an appetizer. Ella chose the sautéed rainbow trout and Grace went for the sautéed coconut curry shrimp and scallops. Ella was excited to share her wedding plans with Grace.

"We put a deposit down on the Whittemore."

Grace clapped her hands. "I'm so happy for you. Brody seems like such a nice guy. You look happier when you're around him."

"He makes me happy," Ella said as their server set their salads down in front of them. "I was infatuated with David. It's different with Brody, I hate being away from him. I think about him all the time and when I see him, I swear my heart races just looking into his eyes."

Grace held her glass up. "To Ella and Brody." She sipped her water and began eating her salad, lost in thought. "I'm thinking about stopping in to see Jimmy on my way home, Sunday night."

Ella pulled the fork back out of her mouth. "He would love that. I'll bet his daughter is so cute."

"Tell me about the Whittemore, why did you choose it?"

Ella glowingly told Grace about the gardens, statues and the bridal suite. "Here let me show you." She held her cellphone up for Grace to see.

"Ella, this place is gorgeous. The waterfall is spectacular. The landscaping is impeccable. Ava is going to love it and I'll bet she gives it her stamp of approval."

"I think so too," Ella said as she pushed her empty plate to the side. "I'm starving."

Their server came back with their dinners and both women were impressed. Ella took back her cellphone and told Grace. "We're having our ceremony." She held her hand up. "I want you to be surprised. You'll just have to wait."

"Fine," Grace replied and began eating her dinner. "Have you decided on a color scheme yet?"

"No, I'll let Ava take care of that and she can pick out—"

Grace looked over at her. "It's okay, I know my place and the fashionista is way better at those details than I am... any day." She laughed. "Besides, it will give her something positive to think about. But I'm in charge of the bachelorette party."

Ella took a deep breath and blew it out slowly. "I only want you and Ava by my side. I would rather spend a fun night together in the bridal suite. It has a nice lounge area. We can sit by the fire, sip tea and talk about—"

Grace put her hand on Ella's. "Whatever makes you happy."

19

Captain Bill announced the water was calm, making it a nice day for cruising along the shoreline. "We have smooth seas today," he said as he pointed toward the bow.

Jude followed David toward the front of the yacht. "This is another first for me," she said.

"I'm glad," he replied as he handed her a mimosa. "I thought you should explore the coastal towns and quaint homes along the shoreline from the water oppose to the roadways."

"Wow," Jude said as the Bill Pay backed out of the port. A few minutes later, she gasped at the sights: the beautiful homes, landscapes and mansions along Bellevue Avenue. David was standing behind her holding a notepad and a handful of pens. She turned to face him. "This is absolutely gorgeous."

David handed her the notepad and said, "In case you want to make a few notes."

She reached out and took the items from him. "You're so thoughtful. Thank you."

"You're welcome. We'll have lunch at Aurelia at Castle Hill. They offer a very nice vegetarian menu and—"

Jude laughed. "Oh, I'm not a vegetarian. In fact, there's very little I don't eat."

David smiled. "Great, I'll let Bill know and have Cory James prepare the Jon Boat, unless you trust me enough to ride on the back of the jet ski?"

She offered a sheepish grin before telling him. "I have to wear a life vest, right?"

He nodded. "We both do." David's cellphone rang. "Excuse me for just a moment." He answered the call and told his lawyer. "September thirtieth at ten a.m., is perfect. Thank you."

Then he told Jude about growing up in Narragansett. "I had the best life growing up in Point Judith. I got to swim every day, go fishing, jog along the water's edge and go clamming with Aunt Emily."

"You swam in the winter?" She pulled her chin back. "Wasn't it cold?"

David laughingly told her about the Dutch Inn's indoor swimming and how they offered day passes to the locals. "That's where I learned to swim and I had the opportunity to meet people from all over the world. Men and women traveled from everywhere to go fishing right here in Galilee."

"I'm a New Yorker, always have been and never really had the reason or desire to travel elsewhere. I grew up near Albany, until my literary agent convinced me to move to the city. It was just easier to meet with her, my editor and publisher. Now, I have an apartment along the FDR, fifteen minutes away from everyone."

"Along the East River?"

Jude nodded and smiled knowing he was going to say something about her not being able to swim.

"Now I know I need to teach you how to swim. As soon as you have enough information for your book, I'd like to take you up to my cabin and give you swimming lessons."

"It's a deal," she said and pointed toward a home. "Who on earth lives there?"

"Marble House was built by William Vanderbilt. It was a present for his wife's thirty-ninth birthday. We can add the mansions to the list of places to visit if you'd like, but I suggest waiting until the winter. The historical society goes all out for the holidays."

"Less tourists, too, right?" She said as she wrote in her notebook.

"No," David replied. "Splendor and grander. From twenty-foot tress constructed of poinsettias to live Christmas' trees in every room. The mansions try to out-do each other. I promise you it's worth your time."

At noon, Captain Bill announced they arrived at their destination. Cory James held the Jon Boat steady as David held Jude's hand allowing her to step in and take her seat. "Thank you," Jude said to Cory James and David.

David asked Jude if she wanted to sit indoors or out on the patio. "Where would you like to sit?"

"Outdoors, please," she replied and they followed the hostess to a nice table under an umbrella near the stonewall. Jude sat down and said, "I think we're a little underdressed to be sitting inside."

"Not at all," David replied. "Don't let the suit and tie scare you. A lot of people dine in their bathing suits." He tossed his hand up. "They wear a cover-up, but still."

"May I take your drink orders?" Their server asked.

"Jude, would you care for a cocktail?"

"Yes, if you're having one," she said and looked down at the menu.

David looked up and ordered himself a beer. Jude echoed his sentiments. "I'll have a beer as well with a slice of orange on the side please."

The waiter smiled it wasn't the first time someone ordered an orange wedge to go with their beer. "I'll be right back," he said as he set their menus on the table.

"The butternut squash soup sounds delicious, "Jude said as she continued reading the menu. "In the city you can order anything. The most amazing chefs are everywhere. Although, I have never heard of a soup with pecan pie crumble, orange ash and crème fraiche. I need to try it."

After dinner they had the Sailor's Sweet Tea made of white rum, citron green tea and a fresh lime wedge while sitting at a café table waiting for Cory James to return with the Jon Boat.

"David, thank you for such a lovely day. I enjoyed myself tremendously."

"You're welcome. Are you up for a walking tour tomorrow? I have plenty of time before my next project."

Jude studied him for minute. "I heard about you rebuilding an old run-down inn. That was very nice and generous of you. My neighbor to the right of me said you saved the fishing community in doing so. If you don't mind my asking what's your next project?"

David looked away for moment. He didn't want to sound flamboyant or ostentatious. "I want to build a small community for the homeless," he said.

Jude shook her head. "You are the most genuine person I have ever met." She pointed her finger at him. "You better be careful, David Wayne, I may create one of my characters after you."

David chuckled. "I hope he's a good guy and not a—"

"Cardboard," she said laughing. "Oh, he'll be a real person that's for sure."

They both stood up when they saw Cory James docking the Jon Boat.

"Shall we head back?" David asked as he stood up and waved to Cory James.

"David, thank you for everything," Jude said. She leaned in and almost gave him a kiss on the cheek but stopped herself. There was something about him she just couldn't put her finger on yet and she wasn't about to cross that line. She enjoyed his company and, she was eager to see all that Point Judith had to offer.

20

G race pulled up to the restaurant, parked in her usual spot and reached back for the gift bag. As soon as she walked into the bar area, Jimmy set the shot glass down, came out from behind the bar and gave her a warm hug. "You look fantastic," he said.

"Thank you," she replied and handed him the bag. "I picked up a little gift for the boys and your daughter. How are you?"

Jimmy smiled and pointed toward the bar. "Please tell me you have a few minutes?"

"I do," she replied and followed him. Jimmy handed the men their shots and set four bottles of beer down as well. Then he motioned for his assistant to take over.

"Let's sit at a table. Can I make you a drink?"

"Just water, thank you." Grace followed Jimmy over to the corner table and sat down. "I want to see pictures," she said.

Jimmy handed her his cellphone and watched as Grace scrolled through about a hundred photos of his wife, sons and little girl. "She is so beautiful. She takes after your wife. I can't believe your sons are getting so big."

"I know right? I just made a new appetizer. Will you taste it and tell me if it's any good?"

She smiled. "Of course, I would be happy to."

Jimmy walked over to the kitchen and came back with a tray full of snacks. "Try this one," he said and pointed to a clam shell. "It's call Grace by Fire."

She laughed. "Stop. Oh, my goodness. It is delicious. I taste lobster and something hot, like good hot."

"That's why I named it after you," he said and laughed. "Try the pocketbook. It has a variety of vegetables and Chinese noodles. It reminds me of Ava."

Grace took one bite and said it too was delicious. Then she pointed to one of the oysters. "Let me guess, Ella."

"Blue point oysters, cocktail sauce and fresh lemon. The Maine Mussels are a la vodka like my wife."

"I put a bottle of wine in the bag for her. I hope she still likes Merlot?"

"She does," he said and asked if she had time to stop by and visit. "I'd love for you to meet my daughter." Jimmy tapped her on her hand. "I would love to meet your son."

"Small towns will never change," she said.

"No, I ask about you every time I see Ella."

"I can't believe she still comes in here without me," she said laughingly. "I promise the next time I am passing through I will stay longer, but I have to pick Hudson up and get him ready for day care tomorrow."

Jimmy stood up and thanked her for stopping by. "It was nice seeing you. I miss seeing the three of you walk through that door."

She kissed his cheek and waved goodbye. "I'll see you soon, I promise."

Grace got in the car and drove to Steve's house. She was both excited and scared to see him. What if it was all her imagination. Maybe her heart wished for Steve to be as interested in her as she was in him. "What the hell am I doing here?" She took hold of the welcome basket and knocked on his door. She rang the doorbell and waited. When no one came to the door, she set the basket down on the front porch and wrote a note telling him she was sorry she missed him. "I'm sorry, I didn't let you know. It was a spur of the moment idea."

It was eight-thirty by the time she picked Hudson up from Aunt Emily's. "I'm sorry I am so late she said. "I stopped by and saw an old friend and it took longer to say goodbye than I had expected.

"Hudson is fast asleep in the guest room. Do you want to pick him up tomorrow morning?" Aunt Emily asked as she closed the door.

Grace felt horrible. "If you don't mind. Yes, that sounds good," she said and then asked if she could kiss him good-night. Grace followed Aunt Emily down the hall to a large bedroom filled with toys, games and stuffed animals. She stood in the doorway and whispered, "I feel like I am standing in FAO Schwartz." Next to the window was a piano and to the right of that a seven-foot giraffe. To the left of the bed was the sailboat. "That's the sailboat he keeps telling me about."

"David designed that when he was fifteen years old. I surprised him and had it constructed right in his room one day while he was in school." She pointed to Hudson. "I'm not sure who loves it more. Him or David."

Grace looked at her. "You gave him such a remarkable childhood and now you're giving my son the same love." Grace kissed the side of Emily's head. "Bless your heart."

Then she tippy toed in and kissed Hudson on the top of his head. "Good night my handsome boy."

Grace arrived home in time to read Ella's text message. "Text me when you get home."

Grace texted her back. "I'm home safe." Then her cellphone rang. "I texted you," she said and laughed. "You're such a worry wart."

"What took you so long?"

"I stopped by and dropped a gift off for the baby. Umm, Jimmy said you go there a lot."

"You saw Jimmy? He looks great right? Did he let you taste his new appetizers?"

"Yes. I miss going there, dancing and—"

"Me, too," Ella said and then told Grace about Ava's new friend. "So, I called and spoke to Ava's sponsor and she told me that Bradley is the salt of the earth and he is just as infatuated with Ava as she is him."

"Like, Bradley Cameron, Bradley?"

"The one and only," Ella replied. "Can you imagine? Ava dating a movie star. Her sponsor said he's very respectable of Ava and he clearly knows what he is getting himself into with her. She also said Ava has not been using for long. Not to say she won't try it again, but with everything going on in her life and with the two of us, she doubts she'll ever mess up again."

"Praise God for that. How does she know how long she hasn't been using?"

"By her own recovery. I guess she's been doing and saying all the right stuff. Before you tell me, Ava knows how to trick people into believing her story, they tested her urine and they did bloodwork on her as soon as she arrived. Her sponsor said, Ava didn't suffer withdrawals for that long of a period. Sadly, complete recovery for some is more difficult if lasting damage has been done."

"Like what?" Grace asked as she started to get undressed.

"Go to sleep."

"No, I need to know," Grace said. "You can tell me a joke after you tell me about Ava's recovery."

"Some people suffer severe damage to their inner organs even brain damage. Opioid overdoes are serious."

"Thank God, you were with her that night," Grace said. "I'll pray for her and ask God to heal her from the inside out."

"Grace, Ava had another seizer last week. It was only a petit mal seizer." Before Ella could explain, she heard Grace crying. "Hey, it wasn't that bad. They said if you weren't looking at her you never would have known she was having one. It was so brief they don't even think Ava realized she was having one."

"How long will she suffer from them?"

"They're more common in children then they are in adults." Ella blew a long breath into the phone. "She just blanks out for a few seconds and stares into space."

"I'm sick to my stomach," Grace said and went into the bathroom. She stood in front of the mirror looking at her reflection. "What can we do to help her?"

"Just keep her as close to us as possible. Hopefully, they can treat them and they go away in time. Grace?"

"Yeah," she replied and put toothpaste on her toothbrush.

"I was at the park yesterday wondering why this Frisbee kept getting bigger and then it hit me."

Grace laughed aloud before saying, "I love you. Good night, Ella."

21

For three days straight it rained in Point Judith, so David and Jude had to cancel their plans. He took the opportunity to go up to the cabin and work on his sketch for the new development. He was sitting near the kitchen window watching a gentler rain fall on the lake. It amazed him how many people still walked along the beach during rainstorms, thunder, lightning, and severe winds. One day, he watched three women run as the swash carried sand particles onto the shore, blasting it in their faces.

He got up and poured himself another cup of coffee. He wondered if Jude was writing or working on her new book series. Before he started working on his drawing, he logged on to the Books-A-Million website and ordered three of her novels. He had them shipped to the cabin so he could read them out on the front porch. Sitting in the glider on cool afternoons with only the sound of birds in the background, a good book and a cup of coffee or shot of bourbon was one of his favorite past times.

He closed his laptop and opened his sketchpad. First, he drew the main road giving himself plenty of room for expansion and hopefully a few more vendors. He wanted the homes to be in one section and the commercial buildings to be at the entrance. The grocery store would occupy the most space, followed by the drug store. David allowed them to be first in line as you entered the community. He was delighted when Grace got both the pizzeria and the deli owner onboard. Once Aunt Emily told a hairdresser and barber shop owner they would have first right of refusal, they both asked where they could sign up.

Tuesday, David was in the diner when the waitress told him she had always wanted to open an old fashion diner offering comfort food. When David offered her the opportunity to be a part of the community, she almost screamed she was so excited. David liked her, single, hardworking, mother of two. He remembered reading in the first chapter whereas women of color are usually never denied funding. "I'll give you the same deal as all my other vendors, free rent for one year and I'll give you a book on government grants that may help you with funding your dream." She hugged him, thanking him and promised to serve every person with the dignity, they deserved. She insisted on buying his breakfast. "I'll drop the book off to you next Tuesday," he said and left her a very handsome tip.

David wanted more for these people. He wanted them to have some of the luxuries he had growing up. He sketched in a swimming pool with a wheelchair ramp, a community room that would allow the men and women to play cards, shoot pool or watch television together.

Behind the houses, David drew hiking trails that traveled along a garden, a park area for people to walk their dogs, or attend concerts. He wanted easy living for everyone. "Everyone? No." David thought for minute. Then he wrote down rules to abide by. Everyone must be homeless, a veteran, disabled or on a fixed income below the poverty level. "I want to create a compassionate community for people to live their best life." He thought about Red and the woman he hired to work at the inn when he first opened. She was in her late fifties, recently widowed and living on the street when she applied for work. David appreciated her honesty and hired her immediately. Today, she is one of his best workers.

Friday morning David woke to clear skies, warm temperatures and a new purpose. He headed back to the beach house to meet with Jude and show her why Point Judith is so special to him. He was just about to head on over to Jude's when he heard a frantic man knocking and yelling at his front door. Red was holding a woman in his arms. "Mr. Wayne can you please drive us to the hospital?"

David rushed to help Red carry the woman to his Tahoe. Red sat in the backseat with her. David drove as fast as he could. "What happened?" David asked as he turned onto US-1 South. "Should I call 911?"

"No time," Red said. "I think she's having a brain aneurysm."

David looked at him in the rearview mirror as he listened to the woman cry out in pain. "Okay, just a few more minutes." David drove the same roads as Shelby had when she raced to get him to the hospital to see Aunt Emily.

David pulled up to the emergency department, parked the car and carried the woman inside as Red told the nurse the woman had a sudden severe headache, blurred vision, neck pain and her left cheek was numb. At that moment the woman became nauseous and confused. The nurse and a doctor sat the woman down in a wheelchair and escorted her down the hall.

The woman behind the desk asked if either of them were the woman's family. "Friend?"

David shook his head. Red told her he was walking down the street when he saw the woman keel over. "One minute she was walking toward me, smiling and the next thing I knew she dropped to the ground. I bent down next to her and asked if she was okay, that's when she said her head just started pounding. When she said she couldn't see, I picked her up and carried to Mr. Wayne's house."

David placed his hand on Red's shoulder. "Please call me David." He looked at the woman. "Thank God, Red was there."

"And you were home," Red said and then asked if he could leave.

The nurse assured them they would take care of her and locate her family. "Would you like me to give her your name?"

"No," Red said in a stern voice. "I'm just glad we were able to get her here in time." He turned to leave. "Thank you, David."

"Red, I'll give you a lift. Let me leave my number in case she needs a ride home." He winked at the nurse as he gave her his name and number.

Outside, Red told David he could walk back to Point Judith. "I can walk from here."

"No, I insist you let me give you a ride. We both know Grace will have my head if I let you walk back."

Red grinned as he got in David's Tahoe. "Thank you and no I wouldn't want to see you get into any trouble with Grace."

Red listened as David spoke about his new project. "Grace has been such a big help to me. Am I allowed to tell her about today?"

"You can do whatever you feel you need to do, but I—"

"You were a wonderful, thoughtful and powerful blessing to that woman. Grace will be so proud of you. I know I am." David turned on Boston Neck Road. "Where can I drop you off?"

"Anywhere is fine," Red replied and got out of the vehicle at David's house. "Thank you for the ride," he said as he shut the door.

"You're welcome. Enjoy your day and." David pointed his finger at him. "You saved that woman's life."

Red offered a quiet nod, turned and walked away. David stood there shaking his head. He went inside and called Grace. After he told her what happened, Grace told David about Red saving the little girl. "I wish I knew him better," David said. "Did you talk to him about the new community?"

"I tried to but you know Red. He's content living his life as—"

"Not as long as I am alive," David said. "I'll work on him. Hey, I'm off to play tour guide for the rest of the day. What are you up to?"

"I have a house to show at two and then yoga before I pick up Hudson. I heard you're having lunch with Aunt Emily next week."

"Huh, I said I would but she never told me when. I guess I am." He laughed. "I'll call her tonight and nail down the day and time. Thanks for the head's up." David hung up the phone and walked down the beach toward Jude's.

22

J ude was sitting outside in an Adirondack chair reading when David approached. She waved to him, set the book down and stood up to greet him. "Hi. Thanks to you I decided to step out of my comfort zone."

He pointed to the sky. "It's gorgeous right?"

"Yes, and finally we can get outdoors." Jude motioned toward the water. "Are they?"

David chuckled. "All the time."

"I almost yelled I can see you," she said and laughed. "But obviously, I didn't." She waved them off and said, "Get a room."

"Okay, we can check that one off our lists," he said. "Do you have time to go for a walk?"

"Yes, but first let me give you my number," she said and motioned for him to follow her inside. "If it didn't stop raining, I was going to ask your aunt for your number when I meet with her for lunch next week."

David held the door open for her and said, "You're meeting with Aunt Emily next week too?" He shook his head. "I'm afraid to say my aunt may be playing matchmaker."

Jude stepped inside, laughing. "Oh, this sounds like fun. I think we should play into it. Enemies to lovers."

"What?" David said a little louder than he intended and then laughed. "Wait, what?"

Jude picked up her cellphone and asked for David's number, then she texted him so he would have hers. "We'll both go to lunch. I'll pretend to hate you and you'll do the same. Yeah, maybe that's a bad idea."

David chuckled. "Why is that?" Wondering how she felt, because if she wasn't on her way back to New York in a year, he could see himself falling for her.

"Tropes," she said. "In romance novels... enemies eventually fall in love."

"Hang on," David said, knowing Aunt Emily saw him looking at her at Dr. Ferris's party. "She'll know we're messing with her. What if you pretend to hate everything about me?"

Jude tilted her head, squinted and pointed her finger at him. "Umm, I'm not very good at lying. I can write about a person not liking someone, but face to face that's too different. Not even I can pull that one off."

David agreed with her. "Let's see what she's up to when we get there. Shall we take a walk?"

"Definitely," she said and put her cellphone in her pocketbook.

David headed toward Great Island Road. "If you're looking for great seafood, George's of Galilee and Champlin's both serve fresh seafood."

"You're making me hungry," Jude said as she pointed to George's.

"Yeah, if your characters are young and festive, they will

want to sit topside. The vibe is upbeat and the views are spectacular."

"How's the chowder?" she asked.

David held his finger to his lips. "Shh, Aunt Carrie's has the best chowder in the world." He pointed to Narragansett Bay Lobster. "If you're looking to host a clam bake, you'll want to get your lobsters from them."

"How about dancing?" she asked as they walked past the US Coast Guard Station toward Ferry Wharf Fish Market.

"Are they young and hip? Send them over to Alchemy in Providence. It's a dance club for the young at heart." He laughed and held his hands up in the air. "Not that I would know." He stopped walking and asked her if she would like to try the best fresh seafood salad she will ever taste. "If you like fresh seafood, you have to try their salad and my favorite smoked trout."

"Oh, David. My mouth is watering. Yes, please."

David held the door open for her. They took their lunch with them and sat outside the Lighthouse Inn. "Across the street is the ferry to Block Island. There are also fine art galleries, museums and as you know the finest historical landmarks to visit. Your characters can also go whale watching, canoeing, kayaking or paddle boarding."

Jude set her fork in the paper box and then in the brown bag. "Point Judith has so many activities and—"

"Oh, I'm not done. They could play golf, go skydiving, horseback riding and—"

"Wait," she said and took out the notepad he had given to her. "I should be writing all this down. You know I could have Googled everything, but this is so much better. Seeing Point Judith is surreal. "It's so beautiful, captivating and peaceful. The city is exciting, but it doesn't compare to this." She waved her hand out in front of them. "I worked on my outline for the new series, thanks to you." She tapped him on his leg. "What did you do in the rain?"

David looked out toward the water, thinking about his community. "I made a sketch of my ideas to show the engineer for the development I am building for homeless people."

"David, that is very admirable of you. Wow, you amaze me more and more every time we are together."

"I'm not sure I am worthy. I just try to do the best I can with all that I have been blessed with."

She pointed to the inn. "I read a newspaper article whereas the reporter declared you as someone who wasn't happy unless he was doing something nice for someone else. I'm starting to believe that. I would love to hear more about your project."

David told her about his idea and about the soup kitchen he named after his aunt. "If you saw the line of people waiting for a simple meal, you would feel the same."

"What's the name of the soup kitchen?" she asked wanting to donate in his honor for helping her write her new series.

"Auntie Em's, it's right down the road." He turned toward the inn and said, "When I bought the inn, it had a lot of stainless-steel equipment still in good condition. That's when the idea hit me. Aunt Emily made a huge donation to the swimming pool and I wanted to give her something back."

"So, you started a soup kitchen. Wow, if only more people thought the way you do. I write a check to St. Jude's every year and think I've done my duty for the year, but you go beyond the scope of philanthropists." She shook her head in amazement. "I need to write a bigger check this year. Hell, I need to do more... a lot more."

David reached for her garbage and asked if she wanted to continue the tour. "Would you care to go coastal shopping?"

Jude stretched out her legs, stood up and said, "Coastal?"

"Come on, I'll show you." David brought her in to see Ava's line of clothes. "This is where I bought your bathing suit."

Jude was in awe of Ava's designs. When she ran her fingers down a pair of Ava's famous pants, David pointed to them and motioned for Jill to wrap them up.

Next, he took her to the taffy shop, where she bought two bags, one for him and one for herself. "We'll snack on them together at seven o'clock every night."

"Okay, I'll be thinking of you the whole time I am picking taffy out of my teeth," he said jokingly.

23

August 21st, Aunt Emily set the table out on the back terrace. She used her finest linen. One of her all-time favorites for entertaining outdoors—her Dolce and Gabbana-blue Mediterraneo linen placemats, matching napkins and serving dishes. On the serving table sat a large vase filled all white flowers and in front of each person's setting a silver cachepot filled with delicate white sweet peas. For lunch, Emily was serving a pitcher of Negroni Spritzer, butternut squash carbonara, chicken Provençal with an almond rice pilaf, and for dessert she made an apple crostata.

At noon, David and Jude entered the kitchen to find Aunt Emily pulling out a tray of popovers. "Oh, you both arrived at the same time," she said. "Good, David, I'd like to formally introduce you to Jude."

They both laughed. "Aunt Emily, Jude and I have a secret to tell you," David said as he handed her a gift bag containing exotic vinegars, imported olive oils, and a custom-made apron. "Open your gift."

Aunt Emily looked at them as if to say what is going on? She laughed hysterically when she read the apron. "Matchmaker." She set it down on the counter and gave Jude a welcome hug. "How on earth?"

David told her that Grace told him about his lunch date and when Jude told him she too was having lunch with her, they knew what she was up to.

"We were going to play a trick on you," Jude said. "But David said it wouldn't work."

"Oh, dear. So, I am exposed." She pointed to the terrace and said, "Lunch is waiting." Then she put her hand on Jude's back and told her that she finished reading her latest novel.

David handed the women each a glass and said, "Cosmo?"

"No, spritzer." Then she shook her hand at him. "You're always up to something. How long have the two of you been talking?"

"David was kind enough to take me on a tour of Point Judith." She sucked in a deep breath adding. "Point Judith has so much to offer. I thought I had it all living in the city, but—"

Aunt Emily smiled like she just won the lottery. When she clapped her hands, Jude knew there something more to learn about David Wayne.

Three days later, David was standing in the window at the beach house looking out at the ocean, when he glanced down, he saw her. "Grace." She was lying on the beach under a big white sun hat, wearing a brown bikini. Her long legs were golden brown from the sun's rays. She pulled one leg up as the water washed over her. David blew out breath as he raised his eyebrows. "Man, what I wouldn't do to find someone as beautiful as her." Hoping she was parched, he grabbed two bottles of water and walked down to the beach. He was just about to say her name, when Jude turned around.

"Because of you, I am enjoying the water," she said with a smile and bat of her eyebrows. "Is that for me?" She reached up for a bottle.

David cleared his throat before saying, "Yes." Then he handed it to her.

"I thought since I am staying at a beach house that maybe I should get a little tan while I am here." She glanced down at her feet. "I haven't been this brown since high school." She held up a bottle of baby oil. "Works like a charm." Then she patted the sand next to her for him to sit down. "There's a whole bunch of kids down by my house. I didn't think you would mind—"

David waved his hand in the air. "Not at all." Then he sat down next to her. He looked up at the sun, inhaled and when he did, he could smell her glistening skin. He couldn't help himself; she was gorgeous and that brown bathing suit made her skin even more appealing. "That's a great color for swimwear."

She pulled the water back away from her mouth before responding. "Thanks, it's old, but I figured it would serve the purpose."

David's heart was hammering his chest, his breathing became even more erratic just looking at her. A couple walked past them, talking about getting lunch soon and David thought it was a great idea. "Would you care to go to lunch? I know a great little place that doesn't mind if you're wearing a bathing suit." He motioned over his shoulder. "I'll make you the best lobster roll you ever had."

Jude sat up straighter, turned to face his back deck and smiled. "I would love that and yes, I am starving." She clapper her hands together. "I love lobster, but I have to tell you I have never had a lobster roll."

24

Grace fell asleep watching an episode of Virgin River. When she woke, she sat up and saw Dylan had also fallen asleep. She had a dream she was living in the house she sold to her client, Steve. They were married with a lot of children. Grace released a long sigh. This wasn't the first time she dreamt about him. She leaned over and said, "I'm going to head home. Thanks for dinner."

He kissed her on the cheek and said, "Okay, I'll see tomorrow, right?"

She offered him a quick smirk and said she was going to Connecticut to help Ella work on her wedding plans. "I'll be away for a few days, but we'll get together when I get back." She got up and told Hudson to say goodbye to Devon and to thank Dylan for dinner. On the drive home, she asked Hudson how many friends he had. "Is Devon your only friend at school?"

"No, all the boys in my class are my friend."

She glanced in the rearview mirror and smiled. "You're so sweet. I'm sure the entire class wants to be friends with you."

"No girls," he said and smiled.

That night, when she tucked him into his bed, she told him she had a surprise for him.

After she dropped Hudson off at day care Friday morning, she headed over to Aunt Emily's to see if she could watch Hudson. "Are you sure you don't have plans?"

"Even if I did, I would change them for Hudson, besides we have a new Lego to put together."

Grace gave her a hug. "He loves you so much and not because you buy him toys, because you spend quality time with him."

Aunt Emily studied Grace for a minute before saying, "Something is not right. You look perplexed. Is there anything I can do to help you?"

"You already have," Grace said.

Aunt Emily raised her eyes and nodded. "Why don't you give me a permission slip to pick Hudson up from day care so you can go take care of whatever it is that is on your mind."

"I'm so grateful to be one of your villagers. Thank you." She hugged Aunt Emily and texted the day care. "They said they know exactly who you are and you don't have to show any identification." Then she showed Emily the message on her cellphone. "Hudson talks fondly about her every day."

Grace was so excited she ran through the house. She packed an overnight bag, grabbed a few bottles of water and two protein bars for the ride. This time she emailed Steve to see if he would be home and to make sure he didn't have any plans for the weekend. She giggled like a schoolgirl when she read his response. "Even if I had plans, they're changed now. I'm so excited to see you. Grace, I'll be waiting for you at the front door."

Her heart raced as she got in her car. Steve reminded her

of a lumberjack, strong, broad shoulders and a smile that made her heart go giddy-up. She remembered the first time she saw him; he was sitting in the bedroom at his old house with a shotgun lying on his lap ready to scare the bejesus out of the first man that entered his home. And when he called her to say he was sorry, she felt differently about him. Knowing his own children would rather live with him and not their own mother meant everything to her. She downed a bottle of water, ate one protein bar and drove straight to his house. When she pulled into his driveway, her heart started beating faster in her chest. Steve was sitting on the porch with a bouquet of flowers on his lap. She gave him a flirtatious smile, parked the car and ran toward the porch. Steve only made it to the first step when Grace reached out for a hug. "The flowers are a nice touch," she whispered in his ear.

He leaned back and said, "I knew you'd get the point." Then he took her by the hand and entered the home. "I have something to show you."

Grace reached out, grabbed his hand and said, "I've missed you." Then she kissed him tenderly.

Steve held her in his arms. "I dreamt about you every night. I used to think you casted a spell on me when you sold me the house and there was no way I was getting away from you." They both laughed at the thought. Then he brought her out to the kitchen and pointed to the cork board with her business card on it. He blushed when he said, "After the kids leave for school, I kiss that damn card as if it were a genie bottle."

"It worked," she said and nodded toward the living room. "I have so much to tell you."

"Can I get you something to drink, eat—"

Grace shook her head. "No, but I do have to use the

bathroom quick." Then she raised her hand in the air. "I know where it is."

He laughed aloud. "Yeah, well don't be surprised if I changed a few things."

Grace came out and sat next to Steve on the couch in the living room. "When I got your first message about introducing me to your children, I cried."

"I'm sorry I made you cry," he said.

"No, they were happy tears. Well sort of. I wished I was still here to meet them and to see their faces when you showed them the house."

"We still talk about me meeting the most wonderful real estate agent in the world. The kids and I are so grateful for that chance meeting." He held his hand up. "No, I didn't tell them their dad was crazy fool and—"

She held her finger to his lips. "Shh," Then she kissed him. "I packed my toothbrush."

Steve looked into her eyes, pulled her in closer and carried her upstairs.

25

David, Aunt Emily and Jude sat in the living area talking about Aunt Emily's book launch plans and Jude's upcoming romance beach series. "How many novels are you planning to write?" Aunt Emily asked as she offer each of them a cup of tea and a slice of crostata topped with homemade whipped cream and a sprinkle of cinnamon.

"Series are hot right now, so I'm thinking anywhere from twelve to twenty-four. Question for you, what is your strategy for hitting the bestseller list before publication? I hold my breath every time I release a new book," Jude said as she accepted her dessert.

Both women have been on the USA and the New York Times bestseller's list, but Aunt Emily seems to hit her mark months before her books are even available.

"I have a great street team; a ton of beta readers and my editor makes sure the right bookstores have a copy six months in advance." She held up one finger. "Oh, and you must include at least a minimum of a hundred influencers."

"Wow, that's a lot of work," Jude said and tasted her dessert. "Oh, yum."

"Jude, did David tell you he is an avid reader?"

Jude looked at him. "No, can I give you one of my books?"

David offered a twisted grin. "You can sign them when they arrive this week."

"Them?" Jude asked wondering how many he ordered.

"Yes, I ordered the first three novels you wrote and after I finish reading them, I plan on ordering the rest." He pointed his finger at her. "If they're as good as Aunt Emily says they are, I look forward to reading them."

"I'm impressed, Aunt Emily said and then sipped her tea slowly. She studied them wondering if David would be successful or not at convincing Jude to move from the big apple to Narragansett. "David, tell me how the development is coming along."

David knew Aunt Emily was trying her hardest to make him look good in Jude's eye, but he wasn't as interested in her as he was the first time he saw her. As much as he liked Jude, he couldn't see himself getting into a long-distance relationship. Besides, she sounded very content with her fast and furious lifestyle. He looked over at Jude, watching her enjoy her dessert, sitting there as if she had been in Aunt Emily's life forever. And yet, there was something about her that said she was contempt wherever she is.

"David," Aunt Emily said again. Then she snapped her finger. "David Wayne, you're doing it again." She raised her eyebrows.

"Sorry, yes. I drew up my first set of plans and brought it over to the architect and engineer to make sure everything was where it needs to be. I think word is out on the project, my inbox is filling up with businesses who want to be a part of the project and I have a few requests from individuals who would like to live there."

"That's great," Jude said and set her fork down. "That was so good. Emily, you must be so proud of David. I know I am."

Aunt Emily grinned from ear to ear. "Who all is interested?"

"I have a pet store, ice cream parlor, but best of all an internal medicine doctor, a podiatrist, physical therapist, oncologist and a neurologist. Oh, and an urologist."

Aunt Emily stood up, clapped her hands and said, "I knew it. I just knew they would all sign up."

"You told them about the project, didn't you?" Jude said and she too stood up. "David, how can I help?" She held her hands in a prayer like position. "Please let me do something. You have been so helpful to me."

Aunt Emily put one hand on David's shoulder and the other on Jude's. "The two of you are so good for one another."

Both Jude and David laughed in perfect unison. "We try," Jude said.

"Oh, wait. Has my cardiologist emailed you yet?"

"I was wondering how everyone got my email address. No." He offered a smirk. "Not yet."

"I have an idea. I could finance the library and I'll bet I could get my publisher to donate all the books," Jude said with a smile.

"That sounds like a wonderful idea and I'll have my publisher do the same," Aunt Emily said.

"David, you should have a waiting list. It builds intrigue and it makes them want to join even more," Jude said and Aunt Emily agreed with her. Then she asked if she could take pictures for her Instagram page. "Emily, I need to tell you when my editor said you were inviting me to your home, I almost died. Everyone in the office wanted to come."

"Of course, you may take pictures," she replied. "Would you care for a tour?"

"Umm, yes. Please," Jude said and looked over at David. "This doesn't count; you still have to take me to see the mansions this winter."

At that moment, David's cellphone rang. "Sounds good. I'll wait here while the two of you meander around. Excuse me for one second, I need to take this call." Then he answered his call. By the time he finished speaking to his attorney, Aunt Emily and Jude came back to the living area full of decorating ideas.

"Has David taken you up to the cabin yet?" Aunt Emily asked.

"Noooo," Jude replied. "Not yet, but he did offer to teach me how to swim."

"Ahh," Aunt Emily said. "Yes, David is an excellent swimmer. Well, you're going to love the cabin, David designed it himself. Right down to the décor."

"If you ladies are through trying to play match maker, I have an important meeting to attend."

"I'm sorry," Jude said as she hugged Aunt Emily goodbye. "It was so nice of you to play match maker... with me and David." She laughed aloud. "Too bad someone doesn't like playing games. Seriously, please let me know when you're in Manhattan, I would love to take you to lunch."

David kissed Aunt Emily and told her he had to meet with his attorney one more time before the closing. "Allan said we need to go over a few things, he wouldn't explain only that it was important and the window of opportunity was about to close. Whatever that means."

As soon as Jude and David got in the car, David asked

Jude if she had time to stop by his attorney's office. "By any chance, do you have time to go with me?"

"Absolutely," she said and fastened her seatbelt. "I love Aunt Emily."

When she called her aunt, David grinned knowing his aunt was working her own magic on Jude.

Allan explained there was an easement on the property that needed to be dealt with prior to closing. "The seller forgot to mention one critical selling point to us. The land buffers a swamp."

David knew exactly what that meant. He ran his hands through his hair. Jude looked at him intently. David looked at her and explained. "You can't build next to protected land."

"Oh, David, I am so sorry," she said.

Allan sucked in a deep breath. "What if you put the surrounding land in the conservancy?"

"Is that an option?" David asked, hoping it was and it didn't require too much property.

———————

26

Grace spent two glorious days wrapped up in Steve's arms. When he introduced her to his son and daughter, she wanted to cry they were so welcoming. His son showed her the secret room in the house. "I had no idea this was even here," she said.

"Come inside, look for yourself," Mal said and Grace followed him through the opening.

When Maddie asked Grace if she could stay for her dance recital, Grace bent down and told her she was honored to be asked. "Thank you so much for asking me."

"Can you bring Hudson, too?" Maddie said and clapped her hands. "Please?"

Grace looked over at Steve. He was smiling and giving her a thumbs up. "Hey, I know. Why don't we let Grace breathe for a few moments before we—"

Grace hugged Mal and Maddie. "I'm fine. I've never been happier in my life. I'll go back to Point Judith, grab Hudson and see all of you on Wednesday."

Maddie hugged her. "Yay, you'll be here for recital on Friday."

Steve walked over to them and gave them a family hug. "Jimmy will be so surprised to see you," he said and smiled.

"Oh, yeah. You can come to the birthday party with us on Saturday. We'll introduce Hudson to all the kids, "Maddie said.

"Okay, kids it's adult time. I want you to do your chores and play outside for a while."

"Okay, Dad," Maddie said and nudged Mal on the shoulder.

Grace and Steve sat out on the front porch. "I'll miss your pillow talk tonight," he said.

Grace looked over her shoulder, got up and sat on his lap. "Can I take you and the kids back with me?"

"We can live wherever you want," he replied and kissed her long and hard.

Tears streamed down her face. "I'll be back before you know it and just so you know." She kissed the tip of his nose. "I love this house."

"House?" he said out loud and pushed her off his lap. Then he pulled her back and said, "I love you, Grace Sammon. From the first day I set eyes on you."

"Thank you," she teased and laughed before saying. "I love you, too." Grace said goodbye to the kids and to Steve. When she looked in the rearview mirror, she could see Maddie crying. Grace slammed on the brakes, got out and dropped to her knees, holding her arms out to her, Both Maddie and Mal ran into her arms and hugged her neck. Grace had tears in her eyes. "I promise, I will be back and we will be—"

"A family?" Mal said.

"Yes, sweetheart. A family."

Mal wiped his eyes and ran to his father. Steve picked

him up and told him. "I feel the same way." Then he walked down the driveway and told Maddie Grace needs to leave. "Maddie, if you want to meet Hudson, you need to let Grace go, honey."

Grace spent the most remarkable weekend she had in a long time. This time, she felt the adoration of a family and the need to love and be loved. Driving back to Point Judith felt like forever, she wanted to turn the car around and run into his arms and never leave.

As soon as she reached her house, she teared up knowing what she had to do next, the people she had to say goodbye to and the home she needed to put on the market. Point Judith served its purpose. She went inside and called Aunt Emily, just hearing her voice brought tears to Grace's eyes. She loved Aunt Emily. "Okay, I'll be there in twenty minutes," Grace said and had to hang up the phone. Grace sat on the floor, brought her knees up to her chest and hugged them. She was worried how Hudson would take the move. He loved Aunt Emily; she was like a grandmother to him. She got up and headed to Aunt Emily's.

Hudson ran to her. "Mommy, come and look at my new Lego Town."

Aunt Emily gave Grace a hug and said, "He's getting very good. Any day now, he won't be asking for my assistance."

Grace's heart skipped a beat. Her eyes filled up fast. Aunt Emily asked Hudson to please go out to the kitchen. "Hudson, why don't you go and have your afternoon snack and tell Maria to take you down to the Victorian greenhouse and show you all the lemons."

"Can I pick one?"

"You can pick a whole bunch," she said and blew him a kiss.

Grace followed Aunt Emily to the back terrace. Before they sat down Aunt Emily gave a warm hug. "You can tell me anything," she said and wiped away a tear on Grace's cheek.

"I'm in love," Grace responded and sat down.

"That's wonderful," Aunt Emily said and then asked. "It's not with Dylan, is it?"

Grace shook her head. "I met him before I met Hudson's father. It's a long story but we somehow made a connection and the feeling is mutual."

"I'm guessing that's the reason you went away this weekend."

Grace blew out a breath. "He lives in Connecticut."

Aunt Emily turned to face the Victorian greenhouse. She stood up, crossed her arms over her chest and took in a breath of her own. "I wish you so much happiness." Then she turned around and said, "I will visit Hudson often."

"Absolutely," Grace said and stood up. "Aunt Emily, I can't thank you enough for all that you have done for both Hudson and me. I give you my word, we will spend our summer vacations in Point Judith." Grace gave a head tilt. "I won't sell the house; we'll keep it so we can visit you and Uncle David."

"When do you leave?" she asked.

"I don't know. My heart wants to leave as soon as we can, but I know I have a lot to do before we can go."

Aunt Emily shook her head at her. "You listen to your heart. Don't worry about anything or anyone. You go and live your life." She put her hands on Grace's shoulders. "Your happiness is all that matters. If it's okay with you, I'd like to keep Hudson overnight."

Grace swallowed the lump in her throat. "He can miss

day care tomorrow. I'm sure he would rather spend the day with you then—"

Aunt Emily hugged her for several minutes. "It's okay." She pushed her back, and looked into her eyes and said, "He's young enough to adjust and as long as that little boy has his mother, he has everything he needs."

Grace gave her a rueful grin. "I hope you're right. I suppose I should go and tell David."

"That won't be easy. I know the bond the two of have, but once a brother always your big brother," she said and waved Grace off. "I have to get ready for my dinner date."

Grace got in the car and texted David. "Are you at the beach house or cabin?"

"I'm up at the cabin. Do I need to come down off the mountain?"

"No, I'll come to you."

Grace backed out of Aunt Emily's driveway. Stopped the car and looked over her shoulder. The house was enormous, but not as big as Aunt Emily's heart. She inhaled the sweet salt air knowing she would miss it. Then her cellphone rang and she saw it was Steve and her heart came back to life. "Hello, handsome."

"Hey, I was worried about you. Are you there yet?"

"Yes. I'm sorry, I forgot to text you when I got here. I'm on my way to say goodbye to David. Aunt Emily is keeping Hudson overnight, while I pack up our clothes and essentials."

"Let me if you need me to do anything. Just so you know Maddie and Mal have been preparing Hudson's room all afternoon."

"That's so sweet," she said. "Steve, thank you for opening your heart and—"

"Loving you. Grace, I plan on showing you my love every day."

"Oh, my God," she said into the phone.

"What?"

"You just gave me goosebumps."

He laughed. "That's good, right?"

"Oh, yeah. Okay, I'm driving up to David's cabin."

"Grace, tell David, I said thank you for taking care of you when you needed it the most."

No tears, only happy thoughts as she pulled onto Ocean View Highway toward Shore Road. "Steve, I know I told you that David was like a brother to me, but I also want you to know that we never slept together. In fact, I have been alone the entire time I have been in Point Judith."

Silence. Grace heard him clear his throat. "Steve?"

"So, that's why you made love to me three times in one night."

"Stop, I didn't hear any argument coming out of your mouth," she teased him remembering when he woke her up Saturday morning with sweet kisses on the back of her neck. "I'll call you when I get home. If you're lonely, let me know." She giggled. "I learned a new word."

"I'm afraid to ask," he said.

"I'll sext you as I'm getting ready for bed."

"Bye sweetheart."

Grace pulled up to the cabin and waved as David came out holding a book in one hand and a bourbon in the other. He set everything down and met her as she opened the car door. "Hey, you," he said and gave her a hug.

Grace pointed to the porch. "I could use one of those."

"Have a seat, I'll pour you one," he said and went back inside. He returned holding a tray with her bourbon, the bottle and a charcuterie board filled with all her favorites:

stuffed figs, pecans, brie, he even had honey for her to drizzle on her fig.

Grace set the book down and smiled. "Huh, I know this author. She's very good. You're the best," she said and took a big gulp of her cocktail.

"Okay, this is serious," he said and sat down next to her. "Is everything okay with Ava?"

Grace emptied her glass, held it out for him to refill it and said, "Ava is great. Grace on the other hand is moving back to Connecticut."

David looked out at the lake remembering the first time he brought Grace up to see the cabin, he offered to stay there so she could stay in the beach house for the summer. He would have given her the moon if she asked for it. He filled both of their glasses, held his up and said, "I knew when you went to visit Ella and Ava you would be going back."

"David, I'm not moving back to Connecticut for them. I'm in love and Steve has asked me to move in with him and the kids."

David held both hands up. "Wait, the guy you sold the house to? That Steve?"

"Yes, that Steve," she said knowing he would feel that way. "I know what I am doing. He makes me happy; he loves me and I love him."

"That's all that matters." He shook his finger at her. I want to meet him and I better be the one to give you away."

Grace's eyes filled up fast. "I love you so much. You will always be in our lives. I promise you; we will come back every summer just see you and Aunt Emily." She started to cry.

David pointed his finger at her. "They better be happy tears. Grace, I love you more than you know. I could not have built the inn without your help. Every time I step foot in one of those rooms, I am reminded of your design, love and support."

"And every time I think of Point Judith, the beach and —" Her tears turned to sobs. David stood her up and held her in his arms.

"He better know the treasure he has in you."

S eptember brought so much joy to Aunt Emily, David and to Grace. Because of the children, Steve and Grace decided to elope. Hudson stood next to his mother holding her hand, while Maddie held Grace's bouquet, and at the right moment, Mal held up their wedding rings. The ceremony was held at Steve's pastor's home. As soon as Grace saw the dock, she knew she wanted to get married outdoors. The lake made for a perfect back-drop. Blue skies casting over the lake enhanced a glow creating blue water.

On the second Tuesday of the month, Aunt Emily's book was released. Everyone was at the celebration, even Ella. She introduced Brody to Aunt Emily and to David. Shelby captured the moment perfectly. "Come on everyone smile," Shelby said as she motioned for everyone to stand closer to Aunt Emily.

In true Emily fashion the room was filled with food, signature cocktails and party favors. First, a meet and greet. Emily stood up and introduced herself to everyone and thanked them for coming. Then she had her assistant pull back the curtain exposing the table filled with signed, first edition copies of her cookbook. Everyone applauded when she shared her favorite recipe in the book. After a brief Q & A session, Emily read some of her most precious moments aloud. "On page one hundred is a photo taken of me and my grandson, Hudson. As you can see, we are baking his favorite cookies. I encourage you to spend more time in the kitchen with your children and grandchildren. Treasure every moment, recipe and kitchen disaster."

Everyone laughed.

Emily's assistant asked if anyone wanted a photo taken with Emily. "Chef, Emily will be taking pictures for the next fifteen minutes," she said and motioned for Shelby to start with Emily, Hudson, Maddie and Mal.

One person raised his hand and asked if all the food being served was from the cookbook. "Are these in the cookbook? Because they are divine," he said holding up a tomato and goat cheese tart.

"Yes," Emily's social media manager said as she snapped a photo of him taking a bite.

"Aunt Emily, when I come to visit you can my brother and sister come too?" Hudson said as he reached up and took hold of her hand.

Emily bent down, kissed him on the cheek and said, "I already asked your mother and your father if the three of you could spend a whole week with me at my beach house."

All three children clapped. Steve winked at Aunt Emily and told the children to head on over to the photo booth so he could get a silly picture of them wearing a chef's hat and apron. "Come on you guys, let's take a few pictures for Aunt Emily's photo album."

Aunt Emily's assistant motioned for her to stand next to

a group of women who wanted to snap a photo for their Instagram and TikTok accounts.

Jude arrived late for the celebration. She had an important meeting of her own to attend. Her sixth novel was set to be released in March. She waved to Aunt Emily as she made her way toward David. "Hey, handsome. I could use one of those."

David took one look at her and lost his breath. She was wearing a sexy short black skirt and thigh high boots; her hair was tied in a high twist and she smelled so good. "Wait here," he said and walked over to the bar. "Two bourbons, one on the rocks with an orange twist, please."

David approached her from behind, inhaled her fragrance once again. "You smell wonderful," he said as he handed her the glass.

"Thank you, it's new. My editor gave it to me."

"Is your editor a male or female?"

"Female," she replied and laughed. "Why?'

"Because she has good taste." When David looked up, he saw Ella looking in his direction. He thought about introducing her to Jude, but by the time he located her again she was talking to Grace and Steve. David wondered if Ella was just as happy for Grace as he was. He hoped she wasn't mad at her for eloping. Steve seemed like a nice guy and according to Grace, he was perfect.

"Look at you," Ella said. "My God Grace you are glowing."

Grace quickly gave her a curt flick of her chin as she told Ella, "No, I am not pregnant." Then she leaned her head back resting it on Steve's chest, looked up at him and said, "But we're working on it."

"That's right, we need to even the playing field," Steve

said as he kissed Grace on the lips. "We're hoping for a little girl, but—"

"Nothing," Grace said. "You promised. Fine then I want twins."

Ella reached for Grace's hand. "I'm so happy for you."

Grace moved closer to her and showed her some of the photos the kids had taken. "We're framing this one," she said as she handed her cellphone to Ella. It was a photo of Grace and Steve standing on the dock, Steve was holding Grace in his arms as he leaned in and lowered her slightly for a kiss.

Ella scrolled to the next picture and sucked in a breath before saying, "This one needs to be framed as well." It was a photo of Steve and Grace, holding hands, walking toward the end of the dock. "Your butt looks amazing in that dress." Grace was wearing a long, white lace, bare back dress that enhanced her curves... perfectly.

"Thank you, Maddie picked it out." Grace looked over at the kids. They were sitting together eating pastries, laughing and behaving as they should be. "I can't wait for Ava to meet them. Maddie is a little fashionista."

Ella thought for a moment and then said, "Why don't you and Maddie go see Ava next month?" She waited for Grace to answer her, but then added, "I would appreciate it."

"Maybe, Steve and I will go," Grace said and motioned for them to move closer to Aunt Emily.

"You're right, we don't want to shock her with too much all at once. She better be getting out in January because I want to get married on Valentine's Day."

Grace hugged her. "Seriously? I always saw you as a June bride."

"Since when have I ever been traditional?"

They both laughed. Ella watched as David stood next to

his aunt and hoped he found his soul mate. "He's so good to her and she's—"

Grace looked at Ella and then at Aunt Emily and David. "I hope he falls in love soon. It will make her happy to know that he has someone other than her in his life." Lord, I hope my plan is working.

The party ended with Aunt Emily 's staff handing everyone their gift bags filled with samples, a copy of her cookbook and an apron that read, "This is what an awesome CHEF looks like!"

Aunt Emily hugged Grace and Ella, telling them she was happy and proud of the two of them. "I received a letter from Ava, thanking me. She sounds wonderfully happy and upbeat. I pray she maintains that attitude when she comes home. I hear she also found someone to cherish her." She winked. "My prayers are coming true." A smile tugged at the corners of her mouth and her eyes grew a little wider. "The power of prayer can be remarkable." She kissed them before saying, "I love you all oh, so much."

D avid sat at the closing table with a thankful heart. Allan worked out a deal with the department of conservation to protect the ecosystem by putting a five-acre strip along the water's edge into the conservancy. He also ensured them the area would be safe from any building now and in the future by installing perennial gardens all along the water's edge.

When David shared his vision with Allan, he was pleased to see David had applied for several grants. "This will ensure the future of the community for a long time to come," Allan said as he handed David a stack of papers to sign. "Are you ready?"

David picked up the pen and began signing. "I am just as excited about this project as I was to build the inn."

After everyone left, Allan handed David a cigar, moved the chair next to him and asked to see his design. "Did you bring it?"

David reached down and picked up his briefcase and handed Allan the plans. Then he unrolled the foil map.

Allan looked over every detail. When he noticed David

had assigned thirty-six acres for commercial use and fifty acres for the homes he was pleased. "Wait, you put fifty acres into conservation, that's more than they asked for."

"Yes, I included the garden, hiking trail and a small fishing pond to also be placed into conservation. I want to make sure no one comes along and builds any more than we need to," he said and then pointed to the pavilion. "Aunt Emily insist on paying for the pavilion and the swimming area."

"Are you still thinking about installing a wheelchair ramp?" Allan asked as he grabbed his checkbook, tore out a check and handed to David. "I know you don't need anyone's money. I'm proud to call you my friend and friends don't let friends do something this spectacular without letting their buddy's in on it. David, I am so proud to call you, my brother in Christs' name."

"Amen," David replied as he accepted Allan's check and told him he would be sure to put it to good use. "I give you my word," he said and lit both of their cigars.

When David pulled up to the property he was met by Hugh Minor, the Narragansett Times and The Providence Journal. John and his crew stood behind a huge banner. Aunt Emily stood next to Jude who was holding an enormous, oversized bottle of champagne. Someone he didn't know was holding up a pair of scissors. When he noticed the ribbon, he became choked up. He parked the Tahoe, got out and waved to everyone. "Thank you so much," he said and kissed both Aunt Emily and Jude. "You didn't have to do this." Then he shook everyone's hand, thanking them as well.

John and his crew shouted, "Congratulations." as David cut the ribbon.

Much to his surprise, Aunt Emily had cupcakes for

everyone along with hot coffee, tea and cold water. An hour later, David was met by a dump truck, toting a trailer and a bulldozer. A few minutes later, another truck, backhoe and John's box truck arrived loaded with chainsaws, shovels and enough tools to begin construction.

David said goodbye to Aunt Emily and Jude. "I promise we will continue our tour soon," he said to Jude.

"It's fine, I need to go to the city to meet with my editor for a few days. I'll let you know when I get back."

"On Wednesday, I'm also headed to the city," Aunt Emily said. "I'm having lunch with Jude at her penthouse, but I'll be back by Friday."

David gave her a kiss on the cheek and told her he would stop by over the weekend to see her. Then he turned toward John and said, "I better get started before the sun goes down."

By the end of the day, John had the main road graded and ready for blacktop. "Tomorrow, I'll start cutting the side roads," John said as he climbed down from the bulldozer.

David showed the layout to John one more time. "When you're done grading all the roads, let's start with the hiking trail along the perimeter. I want to make sure the black top trucks are in and out in as little time as possible. I'm worried about them driving behind the cul-de-sac."

"Don't worry, I'll have the other four roads in by the end of the week. In fact, I'll have Connor take the backhoe first thing tomorrow morning and start pulling up any stumps and rocks along the trail so it's ready for me next week."

David turned around and saw a small truck pull in. "Thanks, John." He walked over and asked if the driver need directions. "Can I help you?"

"Yeah, I have some signs you need to sign for," the driver

said and got out of the truck. When he lifted the cover David saw his road signs.

"I forgot they were coming," David said as he helped the man take them out.

"So, what's happening here? By the looks of the signs, it appears some sort of military base is going in."

David shook his head. "It's a housing development for veterans and homeless victims."

"Wow, that's nice." Then he read each sign as he handed them to David. "Air Force Way, Army's Way, Coast Guard's Way, Navy's Way, Marine's Way and Veterans' Way to be placed along the hiking trail. I left the note on the sign in case it had meaning," he said as he reached for the sign poles. "Actually, my wife thought it was important enough to leave."

"She was very thorough on the phone, I'm glad you were able to make them in such short notice. I want to make sure they go in the ground before the cement trucks arrive."

"No problem," he said as he pulled the tonneau cover back down. When he shook David's hand he thanked him for his service.

"On, no. I'm not a vet," David said.

"Well, I was," he said. "So, thank you for doing this."

David extended his hand out to him for a second time and said, "God bless you and thank you for serving our country."

He tapped David's hand and said, "It was an honor."

"Wait," David said as he let go of his hand and walked over to the Tahoe. "If you know anyone who has served, is homeless, or has an income near the poverty level, single, married, widowed, please let them know they are welcome here." Then he handed him his business card. "They can call me direct."

"David Wayne, I read about you. My wife said you rebuilt the old inn in Point Judith." He held his hand out to him again and asked if he could take a picture for his wife. "She is not going to believe I met her idol. She prays for you every night."

"How can I refuse," David said. After he took the picture, David told him to thank his wife for her prayers.

"Oh, she'll be praying for your new community, that's for sure." David waved to him as he drove down the road, tooting his horn.

When David turned back around everyone was packing up for the day. He stood there looking at the property. His heart was full. He knew deep down that this was his legacy. He closed his eyes and whispered. "I hope I make you proud."

29

Grace was so excited to go see Ava. "Steve are you ready yet?" she hollered from the kitchen.

"Yes," he said and she jumped. "Calm down," he added. "You're making me nervous."

"Why are you nervous?" She asked as she picked up her pocketbook and cellphone. "Because I haven't told her about us getting married yet. I don't want her to think I am living life without her."

"But you are," Steve responded and opened the car door for her to get in. When he got in the car he said, "Grace, don't you think it's encouraging for her to see life moving forward?"

"I suppose." She turned to look out the window, fastened her seatbelt and turned to face him. "Ava is the planner, she —" Grace turned the radio down. "Ava planned my entire wedding. I don't want her to think I don't need her."

Steve reached over, took Grace's hand in his own, kissed the back of it and said, "Ava can plan the baby shower."

Grace coughed twice as the words stuck in her throat.

"You saw it," she said and slapped his knee. "I wanted to surprise you tonight."

Steve pulled over to the side of the road. "Sorry, but it's not my first pregnancy test." A smile crossed his face.

Grace leaned over and kissed him. "We absolutely cannot tell a soul until I am in my third trimester."

Steve rubbed his hands together and said, "It will be the best Christmas present... ever." Then he put the car in drive. "Hey, how come we only get to visit her for a half hour?"

"Oh, please this place has more rules and regulations than the Federal Register. It's a good idea, otherwise who knows what could happen or who could show up."

"Are we allowed to bring her food?" He asked as he turned onto Route Seven.

"No, nothing. She's not even allowed to have her cellphone. When she writes to me, she must leave the envelope unsealed so they can read it."

"Are you serious?" he asked as he pointed to the sign up ahead.

"Yes. Okay, this is it. Oh, please be in a good mood," Grace said as she freshened her lipstick. "There she is." Grace got out of the car and held Steve's hand as they approached Ava. "Ava, this is Steve and we have something very special to share with you, but first, how are you?"

Ava hugged Grace then she hugged Steve and said, "Congratulations." She winked at Grace. "Shelby was sad to see you leave. I on the other hand am so frigging excited for the two of you. OMG, Grace. Tell me everything."

Steve pursed his lips, sat down and listened to Grace tell her friend everything. Ava cried when Grace showed her the wedding pictures. "I'm so happy for and I love the idea that you moved back home too."

"Really?" Grace asked. "What about Point Judith? The store?"

Ava shrugged her shoulders. "Jill can run the store. I want to be here for Ella's wedding. For the birth of my godsons and goddaughters. I'm not going to miss a single day of your happiness or Ella's."

Grace had tears in her eyes. "We're doing this?"

"Oh, hell yeah," Ava said and then turned toward Steve. "Sorry, we only get to see each other once a month. "So... how on earth did the two of you meet?"

Steve waited for Grace to answer her. When she didn't, he said, "We both fell in love with the same house."

"Tell me everything."

"I have a son and a daughter. Mal is ten and Maddie is nine." Steve put his hand on Ava's shoulder. "I promise you; I will love, cherish and take care of Grace like my life depends on it. My kids fell in love with her the first time they met her."

Grace studied Ava's face. "They cried when I left the house to go back to Rhode Island. I wish we could have brought them with us."

Ava leaned over and hugged Steve. She whispered in his ear. "Thank you for coming." Then she stood up and said, "I better get back inside."

Grace stood up to hug her. "I love you and I will see you next month, wait, how's?" she went to say, but Ava interrupted her.

"We broke up. Grace, it's fine. I'm fine." Ava kissed her on the forehead. "My main concern right now is my health. I need to make sure I don't suffer any more seizures and get back to work. No distractions and believe me, he was a distraction. Steve, it was a pleasure meeting you. Grace hug Hudson for me and tell your stepchildren Auntie Ava will come home soon." She waved her hand in the air and headed for the front door.

"Wow, just wow," Grace said as she stood there watching her walk away. "She's back. The feisty, fearless, fighter is back." Grace closed her eyes. "Thank You." Then she took hold of Steve's hand and headed back to his car.

"I like her," Steve said as he backed out of the parking lot. He glanced over at Grace. "Are you okay?"

"I can't believe she heard about us getting married from Shelby."

"Shelby?" Steve asked. "Grace, Ava didn't say she heard about us getting married, only the fact that you moved back home."

"No, she knew. Someone told her. I'm sure of it." She took out her cellphone and called Ella. "Hey, did you tell Ava about me and Steve getting married?"

"Hell, no," Ella said. Hi. Jesus. I take it you went to see Ava."

"Sorry," Grace said. "Hi. Apparently, Shelby told her in one of her letters that I moved back to Connecticut. And she didn't seem to surprise when I introduced her to Steve."

"Maybe, Aunt Emily or David mentioned it to her. No, you're right it sounds like something Shelby would say. You can't blame her. How was she to know that you waited so long to tell her."

"Now you're making me feel bad," Grace said thinking about her pregnancy. "I need to go. I'm in the car with Steve and I'm starving."

"Ciao Bella," Ella said and hung up the phone.

Steve took hold of Grace's hand. "Where would you like to go for lunch?"

"Wherever, I don't care."

"Okay, I know exactly where I am taking you." Steve took

her to the American Pie in Sherman. As soon as she stepped inside, she was greeted by the smell of home baked pies, breads and the biggest muffins she had ever seen.

Grace ordered the eggs benedict with a side of hash browns and an orange juice. "Let's take something home for the kids," she said and stood up to place her order. "I'll have the seven-grain bread, six cream puffs and an apple crumb pie please."

Steve paid for everything and jokingly said, "Are you sure those cream puffs are for the kids?"

Grace offered a crimson smile before saying, "Fine, I'll eat yours in the car too."

30

It was a picture-perfect day in New England, vibrant, crisp, cool air with brilliant foliage everywhere in shades of deep red, orange and golden yellow. The sun was casting long shadows across the lake. The temperature was holding at seventy all day. David picked up his cellphone and called Jude. "Hi, would you like to go out to dinner tonight?"

"Why, David, are you asking me out?" Jude replied.

"Nope. It's on the tour list," he said jokingly.

"Ahh, business. Sure, what time?"

"I'll pick you up at a quarter to seven. Wait, I'm not sure I've ever seen your front door."

"That's true you always come to the back of the house. I'll be waiting for you with the light on."

David spent the rest of the day at the construction site. It had been a few days since he was there. He blew out a breath in surprise. John had the road signs in, the roads and the hiking path had been blacktopped, and they were working on the central sewer system on one end and the water extraction system on the other side of the property. John approached him from behind. "David, this is the site engineer. He'd like a word with you." John raised his eyebrows.

David's first thought was there's a problem. "Yes," he said and extended his hand out to the man.

"Hi, I'm Clifford Young. By any chance do have one more house available? My cousin fought in Vietnam and he could use a place to stay. I try to help him as best I can, but he refuses any money, my wife is constantly inviting him over for meals and sending home with what he thinks are leftovers."

David put his hand on Clifford's shoulder. "I would be honored to help him. Yes, please follow me. I have a brief questionnaire that needs to be filled out."

The engineer asked if he could fill it out on his cousin's behalf. "By any chance can I answer the questions? If he finds out I even asked—"

"No problem," David said and handed the paper to him. "Here let me put it on the clipboard for you." Then he handed him a pen.

"This is it? Five questions?"

"That's it." David tilted his head.

"Yes, he's a veteran, no he doesn't make more than twelve thousand dollars a year, no, he is not on drugs, and yes, he is disabled. Wow, that's it?" He handed the clipboard back to David. "You are a living angel. This is incredible."

David set the clipboard back in the Tahoe. "Have you had a chance to walk the property?"

"I did and that's why I asked. He loves to play pool, never mind swimming is good for his knees. He still has shrapnel in both his legs."

"As soon as the first house is delivered, I'll give you a call and have you bring him by. He can pick out his own lot. They should be ready by springtime."

David noticed the sun going down. He looked at his watch. He had less than an hour to go home, take a shower and pick Jude up in time for dinner. He was taking her to Matunuck Oyster Bar in Wakefield. In light traffic it would take him less than fifteen minutes to get there. If Jude wasn't ready and he had to wait for her, they would be late and David hated being late.

He arrived at her front door on time. He smiled when she opened the door and waved. She had on a pair of black trousers, high heels, and a white strapless shoulder sweater that accented her shoulders perfectly. David got out and opened the door for her. "You look beautiful," he said as she got in.

"Oh, wait. I forgot my shawl." She got out of the car and ran back inside.

David looked at his watch and waited for her come back out. Five minutes later, she reappeared. "Sorry, I hope we're not going to be late," she said as she buckled herself in. "I saw you check your watch and I of all people know you are never late."

"We're fine, it's only fifteen minutes down the road. How was your lunch with Aunt Emily?"

"Oh, my goodness. We laughed so hard that day. She is an amazing woman. I'm using her book strategy for my next book release. I think she's still trying to play match maker."

"What?" David said and almost missed his turn. "Wait, what did she say?'

"Oh, she said a lot. Mostly, she offered me a great price for my apartment."

"She'll never leave Watch Hill. She loves her house and besides her studio is there."

"Okay, but she said she could use the test kitchen in Chelsea Market." Jude played with his emotions long enough. The last thing she wanted to do was upset her dinner date. "I'm kidding, she said she would never leave you, although she did love my apartment enough to stay there on weekends." David pulled into the restaurant parking lot as Jude told him. "I gave her a key to my apartment and told her to use it anytime she wants."

"That was very nice of you and generous."

"Haha," Jude said. "I made her promise to help me launch my book. I would love to hit number one."

They walked in and were immediately seated at their table. Jude's eyes were all over the place. "This is a very nice restaurant."

"May I take your drink orders?"

David motioned for Jude to go first.

Jude looked over the menu. "I'll have the Sapporo Space Barley with a slice of orange on the side, please."

David ordered a beer as well. "I'll have whatever you have on tap."

"I'll be right back with your drinks."

"This is amazing. They grow and harvest their own oysters and the vegetables are from their own garden. I'll try the oysters," she said. "Oh, and the seafood paella." She turned around to look outside.

David couldn't help himself as her top had a plunging neckline. He cleared his throat, the guttural sound scratching, as if he was swallowing something too big for his throat. Thankfully, he darted his eyes right before she turned back around, coughed into his hand and said he was going to order the same. "Sounds good. You're going to love the oysters. The sauce is a secret house specialty. Do you like caviar?" he laughed at her facial expression. "Okay, no caviar."

"David, just in case you haven't figured me out by now, I'm a simple woman with very little needs and desires." She winked. "And simple taste."

"Then why do you live in a penthouse in Manhattan?" He held his hand up. "I'm sorry that's none of my business."

"My previous editor used to live there. When he retired and moved to Arizona, he gave me a great deal. Don't get me wrong, I love living in the city, I can walk out my door and grab a slice of pizza, attend a live performance, dine at the finest restaurants in the world or I can never leave my apartment and have everything my heart desires delivered right to my door."

"Providence Performing Arts Center isn't that far from me." He laughed. "Okay, so I can't walk to everything magical and Point Judith isn't New York—"

"Are you trying to get me to stay?" she asked as their server set their beers down on the table.

When she reached for her slice of orange her hand brushed along Davids' and their eyes met.

David placed the napkin on his lap. "I suppose I'm just a small-town guy."

"And I'm an uptown girl?"

"I guess," he said and sipped his beer.

"Emily said you traveled for five years straight. What was the nicest place you ever visited?"

"Bali was nice, peaceful and quiet. Italy is as gorgeous as they say." His face lit up, his tone so familiar, as if she shared in his experience. "When the plane flew over Rhode Island, I was the happiest man alive." A small smile crossed over his face.

The server asked if they were ready to order. They gave him their dinner choices and asked for two more beers.

"Do you have plans for Thanksgiving?" she asked.

"No, do you?"

Her eyes opened a little wider. "Let's do something neither one of us has ever done before."

"Ahh, a challenge. I'm on it," he said.

"On what?" she laughed so hard she almost choked on her beer. He realized that was the first time he had ever heard her genuinely laugh aloud—a nice, hearty, bold sound.

He offered her a seductive smile and said, "Your challenge, Jude."

Their dinner arrived on time to save the moment. "Jude, can I ask you about your books. In your stories, there's no—"

"Sex," she said and put her fork down. "No, I write clean and wholesome romance with a little spice."

"Now you're trying to make me choke on my words. I was going to ask you why no one dies."

"Ahh, now I'm blushing. In romance no one is allowed to die."

"But in Chelsea—"

"You actually read my book."

"I told you I ordered the first three. Anyway, in Chelsea, Andy has cancer and he's suffering and yet you keep him alive. Does that bother your readers? I mean people die in the real world."

"And that is why I write fiction," she said. "I get to keep people alive, make dreams come true and teach my fans something new in every book I write."

David ate his dinner feeling mused, mostly to himself. He made a mental note to order her other novels when he got home. There was something else about her that he liked. Other than her beauty, she had brains and she had a big heart.

Jude picked up her glass of water, took a sip and asked, "Who is your favorite author? Maybe I know him or her."

"Robert Galbraith and John Grisham. Before I started your books, I read Colin Barrett, I might order another one of his, he's a good writer."

"I've never heard of him," she said and asked, "What's the title of his book?"

"He's a British author. Wild Houses—a dark comedy about a gangland kidnapping in rural Ireland."

"So, I'm your first female writer," she said and held up her empty glass.

David motioned for the waiter to bring two more beers. "I'm surprised you didn't know Robert Galbraith is J.K. Rowling's other pen name. She wrote a crime series from 2008 to 2018."

Jude picked up her cellphone. "I'm looking that up. You're pulling my leg. Oh. My. God."

She blushed. "So, I was your second choice?"

He laughed as their server took away their plates and set their beers down in front of them. David picked up his glass in a cheers like motion and said, "You're my first romance writer."

Jude raised an eyebrow and tapped her glass to his. She studied his face, body language and thought when it comes to looks David was blessed with a king's ransom. When their server asked if they would like anything else, they both shook their heads. As he set the billfold down, they both reached for the check and when they did their hands touched. Jude felt a quiver go down her spine. David flicked her hand away. "No way, I invited you, remember? This, is my treat."

"Game on, David Wayne," she said with a wink and a smile that seemed to melt his heart.

David pulled up to her house, got out and walked her to the door. He leaned in to kiss her goodnight, but when she dropped her key and bent down to pick it up, he told her to have a good night.

31

Ella was so excited when she tried on her wedding dress. Unlike Grace's wedding, Ella did all the planning. From the venue to the ceremony and the reception, she wanted to keep things simple. She and Brody had decided not to wait until spring, they wanted to get married as soon as possible and when the Whittemore said they could host an elaborate wedding on Valentine's Dat, Ella let out a wordless shriek of excitement. "Oh, Brody, it will be beautiful."

He kissed the back of her hand and told her, "I am the luckiest man alive. Did you go shopping for your dress last week?"

"I did," she said and clapped her hands. "I fell in love with the first dress I tried on. No, I am not telling you about it. You will have to wait and see it on our wedding day."

Brody squeezed her hand. "I'm so excited to marry you. I want to elope like Grace and Steve."

"Sorry, I need Grace and Ava standing beside me when I marry the love of my life."

Brody tipped her face up for a kiss. "I love you so much."

"I am so in love with you and that is why I want my two best friends alongside me." She looked at her watch. "I have to get to the store; I have orders to send out and an entire line of clothes that needs to be hung up.

Brody dropped Ella off at the store so she could finish putting the new winter line on the racks. "I'll see you tonight for dinner," she said and waved goodbye.

Brody got in his truck and answered the call. "Hello."

"Brody," Grace said. "I have good news. We have a bidding war going on. You're about to sell your house."

"Are you serious?" he asked and banged his hand on the steering wheel. "Ella is going to be so happy."

"Okay, I'll let you know when the final bid comes in."

"Grace, thank you."

"You're welcome," she said and closed her laptop. Grace was so happy to be home. Hudson loved his new day care and he was excited to be riding the school bus next year with his brother and sister. Grace cried when Mal put some of Hudson's toys in the tree house for him. At dinner time, they laughed so hard at the stories all three children told. Last night, Steve's eyes filled up when Maddie called Grace, mom. Grace sat in the kitchen, sipping her first cup of tea for the day, remembering the night before. She was standing in the doorway, listening to Mal say his prayers. He thanked God for his new mother and little brother. Grace's eyes filled up remembering. "Dear God, thank you for sending Maddie and me a mother that loves us."

Her cellphone chimed. Ella had sent her a photo of the dress she and Ava will be wearing, along with the coat and hand muff. Grace had to call her. "I don't care how busy you are. I love it. Where's your dress?"

Ella blew out a long breath. "So, you're not upset with me for picking everything out by myself?"

"Ella, your happiness is all that matters. That dress is ideal for a February wedding." The purple velvet dresses have a deep back plunge, long sleeves and a scoop front neck perfect for them to wear their gift—pearls with matching earrings.

"We're all wearing the same jewelry, so don't go buying anything special. In fact, I also bought everyone's shoes."

Grace looked down at her swollen feet and said, "By any chance can you get mine in a wide?"

"Grace?" Ella said and waited for her to explain.

"Please don't say anything to anyone—"

"Oh, my goodness. You're pregnant. Yahoo!" Ella screamed into the phone. "Why do you think we're having a winter wedding? We want to start as soon as we are married," Ella said. "Oh, Grace, I am so happy for you. I promise not a word. How do you feel?"

"Like someone blew me up. Hey, Steve is home early, let me see what's up with him and I'll call you later," she said and set her cellphone back down.

Steve entered the mud room, took his work boots off, dropped his pants on the floor and tugged at his shirt teasing her. Grace got down off the stool and stood there watching him. Her mouth going dry at the sight of him. With every deep breath she took, she grew fonder of him. A glimmer of a smile rose noticing his broad shoulders, tapered waist and his gorgeous long legs. A boyish grin appeared on his face as she motioned for him to come closer with her finger.

Her pulse skittered as she drew in a deep breath. Panting, she whispered, "Make love to me."

Steve moved closer, whispered in her ear, "I love you, Grace. I couldn't work. I kept thinking about you, home all by yourself and I threw my tool belt—"

"Shhh," said and took off her top, before dropping her pants and panties to the floor.

Steve picked her up and sat her on the kitchen counter. First, he kissed her face, neck and shoulders, then he made love to his wife. "Now, that is what I call an afternoon delight," she said.

"I'm thinking with a house full of kids, we have to be creative."

"Trust me, my pregnancy hormones... love your creativity."

32

David thought about Jude's request to do something he had never done before and to be honest, he couldn't think of anything that he hadn't done. He's flown in an airplane, cruised up and down the Atlantic in the Bill Pay, and he's hiked the highest mountains. "That's it," he said and opened his laptop. He looked up the Aurora Borealis. "Huh, ten p.m. to two a.m., best seen from Coldfoot, a former gold mining settlement in the Brooks Mountain Range, near the Gates of the Arctic National Park and Preserve. "Okay, let's see if I can convince her to trust me enough to blindfold her," he whispered to himself and closed his laptop.

David headed out the door to check on the progress at the construction site before calling Jude to see if she was ready for her tour of the museum on Saturday. He stopped the vehicle, jumped out and ran back inside the cabin to grab his briefcase and clipboard. "I need to stay focused and stop thinking about that woman."

He was driving up Route 44, when he passed a cement truck and wondered if it was coming from his work site.

When he pulled up to the entrance, he was in aww. All the roads were paved. Up ahead he could see an electric and power truck. David parked next to a big wheel of wire and waved to his foreman, John. "I can't believe you got all the trenches dug in such a short amount of time."

John held up his work order list. "It's your punch list," he said and pointed to the field on the left. "The central sewer system is going in next week. If we're lucky we can start digging for the underground pipes for the well system before winter. The well driller called and said he may be delayed by a week or two."

"Can we call someone else?" David asked as he put his hard hat on and closed the truck door.

"Not really, besides we signed the contract with him and gave him a deposit. These things happen all the time. We'll be fine as long we don't have a hard winter and a lot of frost." John and David walked down toward the entrance and stood in the middle of the road. "I was thinking we should install a storm water system as well," John said and pointed to the pond area.

David nodded in agreement. "Not a bad idea. Is that something we should do now or will that interfere with our plans to be open by spring?"

"Actually, it will keep my guys going." John scratched the side of his head. "We're at a standstill until the electrical lines are in place." He held up both hands as if to say what do you think? "I can't backfill until—"

"John," David said as he put a hand on his back. "That's why I call you. Where are you planning on putting the storm drain?"

John pointed toward to the east. "Between the pond area and the hiking trail."

"Is there room for it?" David asked as they started walking in that direction.

"No one will even know it exists. The only thing they will see is a few catch basins along the way."

David was pleased with John, the progress, and he had hoped for a mild winter. "If you're all set, I need to meet with the rest of my team," David said, turned around and waved to a white SUV pulling in.

John waved goodbye and headed for his crew to get started on the new storm water system.

David smiled as his personal assistant, publicist and new social media manager got out of the vehicle. He wanted them to see the site for themselves. "Hi, let me grab my clipboard and I'll show you around," he said. Then he showed them a drawing.

His social media manager asked, "Why are the houses so far from the main road?"

David's personal assistant answered her, "All the commercial builds will be at the entrance."

"Gotcha," she replied and David smiled at her style of saying she understands. He liked her she's snappy and very good at using graphics on all her social media posts.

"Unlike the inn, I want to spread the word as far as we can to ensure every homeless person in the state knows they are welcome here."

David's assistant told them about her research and what she had discovered. "As of today, the state of Rhode Island has approximately a little over two-thousand-four-hundred homeless people."

"And how many homes are you putting in," his publicist asked.

David looked gloom when he said, "Two-hundred and fifty." He kept walking as he told them about ensuring Point

Judith maintained a zero ratio. "My hope is to have no one go homeless in our hometown and if the project goes according to plan, who is to say, we can't build more."

David's assistant took over the meeting by saying, "I want to start spreading the word in March, by then all of the construction will be finished and hopefully, the model house will be in place." Then she handed everyone their own folder. "I've mapped out a plan of action and a list of things to say and what not to say. I've also included the form everyone will need to complete prior to being accepted into the community."

"There's like five questions on here—"

David chuckled. "Life is hard enough for these folks. Let's keep things as simple as possible."

"Got it," she replied.

As soon as they left, David drove home and called his aunt back. "Hi, sorry about not picking up your call I was in a meeting."

"I figured as much," Aunt Emily said. "I was wondering if you would like to join me for a Thanksgiving feast the week before—"

"Sounds great," he said thinking about his trip to Alaska.

"Well, that was quick. I was also going to invite Jude in case she wanted to attend."

"I'm taking her to South County Museum on Saturday, I can ask her for you."

"Great, I hope to see the two of you then. Enjoy your day, I need to go. I'm on my way to meet with my editor about my blog."

In addition to the museum, David took Jude to the art gallery on Boon Street. "That was the biggest display I have ever seen," Jude said. "And I've seen a lot of charcuteries in my day."

"I figured today was a good day to visit, it was nice meeting some of the artists," David said as he opened the door for her. "Are you cold?"

Jude flashed a lightning grin. "No, I'm excited," she said. "When I first booked my stay, I thought I was crazy for moving here for an entire year, but then I told myself I would just stay a few days here and there and head right back home to work." She tucked her hair behind both ears. "On the first trip back to the city, I was so unsure of what my future would hold, I was wrong on all counts. I never expected to fall in love with the beach."

David listened to Jude as he drove down the road. She's falling in love with Point Judith. "I'm glad to hear that," he said and turned onto Ocean Drive, a mile out of their way. "The ocean can be very beautiful in the winter. The town places Christmas trees in the sand for people to decorate. No one ever sees them; the decorations just appear."

"I do get a sense of community, everywhere we go. It's nice." She took a deep breath before saying, "I'm starting to take your lessons to heart." She waved her finger at him. "I think you're up to something, Mr. Wayne." Her eyes snap to his so fast he heard her neck crack. "Like taking me to a museum when they have Open House was a nice touch and sharing Christmas on the beach does warm my cold heart." She slapped his leg. "I'm kidding, I love the holidays."

His lips tugged with a slight smile as he pulled up to her house. "I'm glad the beach is talking to your heart. Would you like to go up to the cabin next week for your first swim lesson?"

"Yes, I would," she replied and bent down to grab her purse.

"Great, I'll set the pool temperature at eighty-five?"

When Jude hugged her pocketbook and glanced his way, he turned the ignition off.

"David, I have a question to ask you. I realize it's a slightly insane idea, but—"

"Jude?"

She took in a deep breath before asking, "Would you attend a Christmas party with me next month?"

David raised an eyebrow. "In the city?"

Jude waved the idea off. "It's fine. I just thought—"

"I would be honored to go with you," he said and then asked her, "Is it, Black Tie?"

"No," she quickly replied. "You'll go? Seriously?"

"Yes," he said with a smile. "Just tell me when and I will be there. Would you like for me to drive?"

"Or I can drive. It's at the Glasshouse Chelsea. It starts at four and usually lasts until midnight." She chuckled, "That's not past your bedtime, is it?"

He offered her a smirk, telling her she was funny and then told her about taking her for a ride in a helicopter next week. "I thought about your idea and I think I came up with an event neither of us has ever experienced. How do you feel about riding in a helicopter?"

"As long as you don't ask me to jump out, I'm fine," she said and clapped her hands. "You took my challenge serious. Yay."

Monday evening at six p.m., Jude and David flew to Alaska and then boarded a private helicopter. "We should reach your destination in twenty minutes," the pilot said.

Jude looked at David intently as he held up a blindfold. He tilted his head and said, "It's part of the surprise."

She offered him a seductive smile and took the blindfold from him, removed the headset, put on the blindfold, put the headset back on and replied, "This better be good."

After the helicopter landed, David took Jude by hand and instructed her to stay close. They heard the helicopter wind down and eventually the engine turned off. Jude held David's hand as she followed him up a slight incline. She could feel herself getting warm. Something was happening, her insides were trembling with excitement. Then David turned her around and as soon as he removed her blindfold; both her eyes and mouth opened wider. Then he heard her gasp.

"I lost my breath," she whispered and turned to face him. "It's so beautiful. Oh, David—"

"I'm glad you like it and yes, it is beautiful. I'm so glad we got to see it, together."

"I will treasure this moment for the rest of my life," she said as she placed both hands on her heart.

They turned toward the helicopter, slowly walked in its direction, when Jude heard the pilot fire up the engine, she stopped walking and turned around for one more look. "Thank you," she whispered, reached out and squeezed his hand.

33

After attending Jude's office party, David decided to host an impromptu Christmas party for everyone at the inn. He stayed up most of the night working on the details. He ordered enough thank you cards for every employee along with crisp hundred-dollar bills from the bank. He wanted them to know how much he appreciated them. He was glad the same caterer who served at the inn's grand opening was available on the day of the party. At two a.m., he sent the details to his new general manager, turned off the lights and fell asleep. At eight thirty, he woke up, rolled over and searched for her. David dreamt he kissed Jude. She was sitting on his bed, wearing only a bra and matching black lace panties. She had on the same pair of high heels as she wore to her Christmas party. His heart was beating in his chest as he climbed out from under the covers. He sat on the edge of the bed, dropped his head into his hands. "Do. Not. Fall in love with her," he told himself and jumped into the shower.

He was standing in front of the mirror drying off remembering how happy she looked at her office party. She was in her element, surrounded by her friends, colleagues and the people who make her dream happen on an annual basis. She belonged to the book world. Jude was a writer. She was only in Point Judith for a few more months and then she would be off to the big city. "April 30th, she'll be gone." He tossed the towel in the hamper, got dressed and headed down the beach. No jogging that morning, David was headed to Jude's house to bring her up to the cabin for her first swim lesson.

"Good morning," Jude said as she opened the front door for him.

"Are you excited about learning how to swim?" He asked and accepted a cup of coffee.

"I am," she replied and told him she even purchased a new swimsuit. Jude served breakfast, cleared the table and said she would do the dishes when she got home that afternoon. "I'll do them later; I want to grab my laptop and notebook. Today is going in my new series."

"I'll wash the dishes," he said and proceeded to put Dawn on the dish rag. "I'm glad you took me up on my offer to do some writing while we are up at the cabin," he said over his shoulder.

"Should I pack an overnight bag?" She called out from the bedroom and he almost snapped his neck turning around to answer her.

"It's up to you," he said in a shocked voice.

Jude came back out to the kitchen carrying an overnight bag and her laptop. An hour later, they were at the cabin. First David gave Jude the grand tour, then he checked to make sure Henry stocked the pantry and put all her favorite items in the fridge. "There's plenty of snacks and Bud Light

Seltzer for later," he said as he pointed to the kitchen counter and the large bowl of fruit."

"Aww, you even bought oranges. Is there anything you—"

He pointed his finger at her. "Not until you had your first lesson. You can change in the guest room; it's just to the right of the pool." He knew she was about to say something about his generosity, but he had to stay focused.

"I hope this fits. I bought both bathing suits in case I go back in later," she said as she reached into her overnight bag and pulled out a two-piece black bikini.

David's eyes were all over her suit, he opened his mouth to say something, but no words came out. He headed for the pool house and waited for her. She was gorgeous and yes, the bathing suit fit her like a glove. "I," he took one more look at her. "Perfect," he said and gave her a thumb-up. "I checked the temperature. It's eighty-nine degrees, if that's not warm enough, just let me know."

Jude clicked her tongue on the roof of her mouth. "Are you going to swim in your jeans?"

David looked down and shook his head. "Yeah, give me a minute."

She raised her eyebrows. "Good idea, I'll wait right here." She sat on the lounge chair next to a stack of towels. When David came back, she stood up. "I'm all yours." Her eyes grew a little wider as she mused, mostly to herself, pursed her lips and moved closer to the steps leading into the water. "David?"

"Yes, let me go in first, then I want you to slowly get used to the water. Maybe walk around for minute. Then I'll have you lay on your back." He held both hands up like a stop sign. "I'll be right there to support your body." He took in a deep breath as a smile tugged at the corners of his mouth.

For someone who couldn't swim, Jude knew how to keep herself afloat. She managed to perform the breaststroke and the back float perfectly. By the time David was finished teaching her to use her arms in an outstretch manner along with pointing her toes, Jude was able to go from one end of the pool to the other. "Great, remember to bring your arms down the side of your body. Good. High elbow, Grace—"

Jude sank in the water. David quickly jumped in after her. "I'm sorry about that."

David held Jude in his arms. Their faces were so close she could feel his hot breath. She was breathing hard when she said, "It's okay. I shouldn't have reacted like I did. I don't know what came over me."

"Grace and Hudson moved back to Connecticut," he said as he moved her to the shallow end.

"I'm sure you miss them," she said and began to get out.

David followed her up the steps. "Jude, Grace and I never dated. She lived in my house until she had the baby and then she bought a house of her own. We are just good friends. I assure—"

"David, it's okay. I understand, you were good friends. I thought you weren't watching me and you were talking to her on your cellphone." She shrugged her shoulders. "I got scared."

"Next time, I'll stay in the water with you the entire time," he said and handed her a towel.

Jude dried herself off. "I think you should call her. She probably misses you as much as you miss her."

"Jude, she's happily married. I assure you; Grace and I are just friends."

"Still, you should call her, maybe you're getting a vibe because she needs you, or she has something to tell you." Jude said over her shoulder.

"I give you my word, I will never shock you again while you're swimming in the pool—"

Jude spun around quick. "What? You're going to shock me?" She laughed. "David, I'm fine. We're fine. Are you still planning on working on your website for the new development?"

"Yes, and I hope you're still planning on spending the day with me. I took the liberty of ordering a few steaks to cook on the grill along with lobster tails and—"

"And?" she said as she wrapped the towel around her waist. "There's more?"

"Henry made us a nice pesto sauce to go over his home-made pasta." He hitched his chin her way. "That's all."

"Henry, oh yeah, your gate keeper. "Will he be joining us for dinner?"

David made a funny face as he explained to Jude about Henry's willingness to live alone. "Henry is very happy living in his own little world. He enjoys taking care of the place, he likes fishing, hunting and hiking the trails, but that is all he likes." David adverted his gaze. "He's not much of a people person, if you know what I mean."

"Maybe, I can give him a few books as a thank you for the pesto... which is my all-time favorite dish in the world."

"Yeah, Henry unlike me doesn't read. He does however listen to country music. In fact, he has a vinyl collection that must be worth a hundred grand."

"I can take care of that," she said with a wink and a smile so bright she could have guided the blind. "Do you know if he likes Willie Nelson?"

"Don't we all," David said as he started walking toward the main part of the house.

"Great, I'll ask Willie to sign his book, IT'S A LONG STORY, and the cover of his latest album." She waved a hand at him. "Don't be too impressed, I only know his editor."

"Henry would be so appreciative and maybe even read the book."

34

David drove to Auntie Em's soup kitchen and to the local food pantry to tell them about the new development and to see if he could put up a flyer. He turned down Kersey Road and saw smoke rising and flames shooting out of several windows. He pulled his vehicle over to the side of the road and immediately dialed 911. As soon as he got out of the Tahoe, he saw Red standing on the sidewalk. He appeared to be in shock. David ran up to him and asked if he was okay. "Red, are you hurt? Did you see what happened?"

Red's eyes were on the flames. People ran toward them, someone shouted, "Did everyone get out in time?"

David studied Red's face before answering. "I just got here." Then he moved closer to the building and hollered, "Is there anyone in there? Can you hear me?"

In the distance they could hear firetrucks, ambulance and cop cars approaching. David could hear someone yell for help. He ran to the back of the building to see what he could do. A woman neatly dressed, holding a purse and two shopping bags was standing over a man lying on the ground. As soon as the woman saw David, she called out for him to help her. David bent down and told the man not to move. "Help is on the way. A paramedic will be here shortly. I won't leave you," David said just as a police officer and two paramedics arrived on the scene. "Over there," the woman yelled.

David leaned in closer to his ear and asked, "Is there anyone else inside?"

"No," the man whispered and then thanked David for pulling him out of the building in the nick of time. "Thank you for saving me."

When the paramedics lifted the man onto the stretcher, David followed them to the front of the building. The woman told the police officer she saw a man drag him out of the building and put the flames out with his own coat. David looked at Red, he only had on a shirt and pants. David walked closer to Red to let him know the man was okay and that he was grateful. He also wanted to tell him that there were no other people inside. Red nodded his head and walked away without saying a word.

When David got home, he called Aunt Emily to see if she was still going to Maui with Geraldine for the month of December.

"Yes, Geraldine and I are flying together a week ahead of everyone else. The entire birthday club will be joining us. We plan on doing nothing accept eating, drinking expensive wine and laughing until our hearts can't take it any longer. How about you, dear? Will you be spending time with Jude or heading up to the cabin?"

"I'm not sure what anyone is doing to be honest with you. Aunt Emily, do you think you could work your magic on Red? I'd like to see him move to the new complex. Now that Grace isn't here any longer, I'm afraid he won't listen to me or anyone else."

"Why do you think I have the power to per sway him?"

"I happen to know he has a tremendous amount of respect for you," David said and opened the refrigerator door. He helped himself to a cold beer and when he saw the bowl on his counter filled with lemon, lime and oranges, he instantly thought of Jude.

"How on earth do I locate the man?" She waited and when he didn't answer her, she said, "David, answer me, hello."

"I'm sorry. What was your question?"

"How do you propose I go about finding him?"

"Never mind, I have another idea," he said and told her he needed to do something. "I'll get back to you. I'll call you tomorrow." The call ended.

Aunt Emily shook her head. "Something is going on with that man. Maria," she called out.

"Yes," Maria said, standing in the doorway.

"Sit down dear. I need to ask you about David. Have you noticed anything strange going on with him?"

"No, I would tell you if I did. He does seem to be spending a lot of time running around though, but where he goes is beyond me."

"Okay, I think he may have pushed himself a little too hard with his new project. I'll go see him tomorrow to see if there is anything I can do to help him."

Maria got up to leave but turned back around. "Maybe, he is sad? I was so hopeful he and Grace got together."

Aunt Emily shook her head. "I tried so hard to get those two together."

"Perhaps they were better friends than—"

"Okay, that will be all for today," Aunt Emily said. "Thank you, Maria."

David sent Jude a text asking her if she had any plans for the holidays. "If you're not doing anything for Christmas, would you care to go horseback riding on the beach to check out all the trees?"

She immediately texted him back. "Wow, another first for me. Hell, yeah. Just let me know when. Thanks for asking. Hey, I need to go, my editor is calling. YES. MORE EDITS"

David set his cellphone down, leaned back in his chair and closed his eyes. She doesn't complain when she walks in the rain. She drinks coffee at sunrise and she enjoys kissing under the light of the moon, or so she says. David fell asleep on the couch. When he woke his cellphone had three messages on it. One was from Grace asking him to call her when he gets a minute. Jude texted him to say she would like to take him out for dinner on Christmas evening. The other text was from John saying the model house was supposed to be delivered on January 29th.

David sat up and clapped his hands together. It was all falling into place. The community would be open by next summer. He poured himself a bourbon, opened the folder and read the list of business. The grocery store, drug store had already started construction. He was shocked when he saw Grace had a wellness center and Quest Diagnostics onboard as well. "Oh, crap! Grace, I forgot to call her." He dialed her number, hoping it wasn't too late for her.

"Hi," she said whispering.

"I'm sorry, I just got your message," David said. "Is everything okay? How's married life. Is Ava, okay?"

"David, breathe. Yes, everyone and everything is good.

I'm calling to ask you if you would be godfather to our little girl."

David blew out a long breath. "Oh, Grace. I would be honored. I'm so happy for you and Steve. Yes. When?"

"Thank you," she said and added, "One more question. Ella and Brody are getting married in February and she wants to invite Aunt Emily and—"

"Not, me. Right?"

"No on the contrary. She wants you there. She asked me if I thought you would come and I assured her you would. Right?"

"Of course," he replied.

"Good and you can bring a date. It's going to be at the Whittemore, about two hours from Point Judith."

"I'll book rooms for everyone to stay overnight. When is it?"

"Huh, are you ready for this. Valentine's Day. Invitations are going out soon. She wanted to wait until Ava got home, but I said that was too late to send an invitation."

"How is Ava?" He asked and refilled his glass with more bourbon.

"She's great. Honestly, we spoke to her counselor and her psychiatrist and they are both pleased with her progress. Did I tell you she met an actor and dumped him for Shelby? She said she has never laughed so hard or felt as good as she does when she is with Shelby."

"Is that where Shelby has been? I haven't seen her around much," he said and sipped his drink. "Grace, I really am happy for you."

"Thank you. That means the world to me. I'll keep you posted on the baby news and when we are going to have her Christened. I'm glad it's you, Ava and Ella."

"Me, too, Grace. I love you and I wish you all the best in life."

"Hey, don't make me cry. I'm pregnant, remember. I love you too. We both do. Hudson calls his Aunt Emily every night to say good night to her."

"I'm sure that puts a smile on her face."

"Yes, and she was very happy to hear, we decided to keep the house in Point Judith. I told Ella they could use it anytime they want."

"What about, Ava?" he asked. "Will she be staying in Connecticut or moving back to Rhode Island?"

"I sold her house. Shelby is moving in with Ava, here in Stratford. Jill loves Point Judith, so she'll be running the store from now on." Grace turned around and saw Steve had turned the television off in the media room. "It's bedtime, I'll see you in February."

"Bye, Grace, say hello to everyone."

As much as David never thought he wanted to have children of his own, he missed Hudson. He especially missed having Grace popping in on him from time to time. He went to pour himself another drink but set the bottle down. Tomorrow was a big day. They were framing several of the commercial buildings.

David was up at the crack of dawn, jogging back to his house when Jude came running out of her house. "Aunt Emily is a genius. I did it. I hit number one on the New York Times bestseller list." She ran into his arms. Thankfully for her sake, it was too cold for him to be sweaty.

David picked her up and swung her in full circle. "Congratulations," he said for the world to hear.

"I won't be able to go horseback riding with next week, I'm leaving this afternoon to meet with my publisher to do some publicity for the book," she said, shivered and ran back toward the house. "I'm so excited. I'll call you when I get back."

David understood completely how she felt. He's seen it many times with Aunt Emily, the rush, the thrill of hitting number one and the exhilaration that followed for days on end as she prepared for all the media attention. He continued walking toward his house feeling both sad and happy for her. "Get used to it," he said only to himself.

35

January 29th, Grace, Ella and Shelby picked Ava up from the rehabilitation center. Ava looked like she had just got home from a long and relaxing cruise. "Wow, I dropped off a thirteen-year-old and I'm picking up a thirty-five-year-old," Ella lovingly laughed. "Look at you. You look so peaceful and healthy," she added and meant it. "Seriously, Ava. You look great. How do you feel?"

Ava glanced over at Grace and Shelby and said, "Like a million dollars." Her words warmed everyone's heart from the inside out. "My heart was searching, but not for what everyone thinks it should have been looking for. I no longer need the affection from a man to feel whole, or the approval from anyone else to think I am successful. I'm a good person. I have so much to give. To share. I have a life. A life I want to live."

After a few seconds, Ava looked at Ella and Grace. "I'm sorry," she said in a choked-up voice. "I know I scared the two of you and for that I am deeply sorry."

Ella and Grace hugged her. Shelby stood back knowing

she found her tribe. They shared a beautiful bond. Then Ava reached out for Shelby's hand. "Thank you for believing in me, for your letters, words of encouragement and for loving me like no one ever has. I spent years looking for Mr. Wrong but now I have found my Mrs. Right."

"I love you too," Shelby said in a soft voice and everyone laughed happy tears.

"Seriously, this has been a huge life-changing event for me, a healing, and the discovery of the true meaning of love found." Ava wiped her eyes. "I'm divinely happy and if hell ever knocks on my door again, I'm strong enough to say... I am the devil. Now back off."

"Hallelujah," Shelby said and wrapped her arm around Ava. "Shall we go home?"

"Yes," Ava said and got in the backseat. She waited for everyone to get in the car before saying, "I need to go to AA every day. I want to go. It helps. My counselor already set it up for me. It's three blocks away from the store."

Ella turned around and said, "You can leave for however long you need to go." She smiled at Shelby. "Shelby's not the only one in your corner."

"That won't be necessary, I can go in the evening. The meetings are at seven in the church basement."

Shelby touched the side of Ava's cheek. "Right around the corner from our new home," she said quietly.

Grace and Ella first heard silence coming from the backseat, then they heard kissing. They both giggled to themselves. Shelby cleared her throat. "I have a surprise for you when we get home." Then she shook her head at Ava. "You'll just have to wait."

Ava clapped her hands, looked out the window and blew out a long satisfying breath.

A moment later, Grace's cellphone chimed. She read the

message and smiled. "Ella, guess what? Brody's closing is all set for next Tuesday at nine."

Ella pulled the car over to the side of the road. Hugged Grace and told Ava about her and Brody buying a piece of land and building a new home for themselves. "We want to start and have as many children as God will—" She looked over at Grace. "Tell her."

Grace turned toward Ava and told her she was pregnant. No tears, only happy smiles.

"Congratulations," Ava said and asked if she knew if it was a boy or a girl. "Do you know what you're having?"

"A girl," Grace said and then announced she had to go to the bathroom.

Ava clapped her hands again. "We... have so much to be grateful for. I'm going to have so much fun designing clothes for her."

Ella put the car in drive and drove straight to Ava and Shelby's. Grace didn't wait for her to put the car in park, she jumped out and ran inside.

When she came back out, Ava had tears in her eyes. "I'm home." Then she buried her face in Shelby's chest.

Grace motioned for Ella to follow her into the kitchen. "I'll put on a pot of tea," Grace said.

Ella was on her cellphone asking Brody if he heard the news.

"Yes, my lawyer called me; I told him we are buying the bigger lot," Brody said.

"Really?" Ella cried. "Oh, Brody. I love it. How did you know I wanted the twenty-five acres?"

"Please, a barn, chickens. Besides, we need a swimming pool, right?"

"Yes, with lots of pool parties. Okay, I'm at Ava's. I'll see you tonight and tell you all about it. I love you."

Grace and Ella hugged. Grace told her it was one of the happiest days she had ever felt. Ella's eyes filled up fast. "She looks so happy."

One look into Ella's eyes and Grace too started to cry. The whistle blew and they both jumped, laughed and wiped away their happy tears. They brought the tray out to the living room and listened as Shelby and Ava walked through every room.

Shelby and Ava were standing outside the sewing room when Ava asked, "Who?"

Shelby put her arm around her. "I did." She hitched her thumb toward the living room. "They have been a little busy these days. Do you like it?"

"I love it," Ava said and hugged Shelby before heading to the living room.

Ella and Grace looked at each other. Ella winked at Shelby. "If you need anything at all—"

Shelby nodded. "I got this. Hey, I'm taking pictures on the fourteenth."

When Ella and Grace hugged Ava goodbye, they cried happy tears for her.

Ella and Grace were in the car when David sent a picture of the model house delivered to the community. Grace held her cellphone out for Ella to see.

"Wow," Ella said and flipped through the pictures. "How cute is that?" She pointed to the layout: a living room, eat-in-kitchen, laundry room, bedroom and bathroom. "It's perfect for what he is trying to do," Ella handed the cellphone back to Grace and put the car in drive.

"I miss him," Grace said. "He was a lot of fun."

Ella snapped her neck to look at Grace. "Like a brother, right?'

"Yes," Grace said a little louder than she intended. "It

would have creeped me out if he ever tried to kiss me like that."

Ella blew out a long breath. "It's funny how things turned out. How all three of us are right back where we started."

"Home," Grace said and rested her head on Ella's shoulder. "Oh Ella, this Valentine's Day is going to be even more festive than all the rest."

36

The Whittemore was magical. White lights were everywhere, from the chandeliers to the trees outside. Ella asked for white candles and greenery. She didn't want any flowers, only nature's beauty and the Whittemore delivered. Ella, Grace, Ava and Shelby all spent the night before the wedding in the bridal suite, sipping tea, nibbling on smoked salmon bites, hot hors d'oeuvres and pasties, talking about babies and Ava selling her bathing suite line to Bali.

The next morning, the women joined the men for brunch. Ella and Brody handed Grace and Ava their thank you gifts. The women received a strand of pearls with matching earrings from the Ziegfeld Collection at Tiffany and Co., the men were equally satisfied with their personal initial cufflinks. Shelby captured their smiles, tears and laughter as Brody announced he prayed Ella didn't leave him standing at the altar. "I had a nightmare one of us was at the wrong venue."

Ella asked ahead of time for everyone not to meander through the building, she wanted them to see the Garden room and the Whittemore room together. Cocktail hour was to be held in the Garden room under huge candle globes, and in the reception room elegant décor, stunning table linens, votive candles, white centerpieces filled with lemon leaves, and fresh Meyer lemons. On every table she placed silver gift boxes filled with Godiva chocolates at every place setting.

Back in the bridal suite, Shelby took photos as the women helped Ella get dressed. Ella cried seeing both Grace and Ava standing behind her in the mirror. "Do not mess up your makeup," Ava said as she too wiped away a tear.

Grace walked over to the closet and took her own dress off the hanger. "Ava, let's get dressed."

"Great idea," Shelby said. "I want to get a few more photos of the three of you in here before you go down the hall. Then I want to take a picture of Ava and Grace fixing your dress with that huge fireplace in the backdrop."

Shelby continued to take pictures of Ella as the others got dressed. "Perfect. Tilt your head up slightly," she said. "Great, now stand next to the window and move the curtain ever so slightly to the right. Nice."

A few minutes later, Grace and Ava stood behind Shelby cheering Ella on. When Ella turned to face them, she started to cry again. "Stop," Grace called out to her. "Don't make me ugly cry. Remember, I'm extremely emotional right now."

Ava laughed, "Not me and if we do have children Shelby can—"

"Umm, no," Shelby said. "We can hire a surrogate."

"Sweet," Ava said and pointed toward Ella. "I'll bet you make Brody cry. You are so gorgeous, and that dress is perfect."

They all turned around when they heard a knock on the

door. Grace moved to open it. She cried her eyes out seeing Hudson, Mal and Maddie all dressed up. Grace bent down and hugged them. "You guys look so—"

"Mommy, don't cry," Hudson said. "It's a happy day."

"Yeah, Dad made us promise not to make you cry," Hudson said to his mother. "He also said it's almost time for Uncle Brody to see Aunt Ella."

Grace turned around and saw Ava freshening Ella's lipstick and moved to the other mirror to check her own. She smiled as Shelby snapped a photo of Ella's reflection in the mirror.

"Kids, can you all stand behind Aunt Ella, please. Grace and Ava can you wait over here?" She pointed to an area that was perfect for them to be casted in the mirror as if they were looking at Ella and the children.

Ella looked in the mirror and felt a warm satisfied feeling appear on her face seeing her best friends in their purple velvet dresses. She mouthed the words you look beautiful and Shelby told her to say it aloud. "Oh, my goodness, say that again."

Ella smiled as she said, "You both look so beautiful."

"That's it," Shelby said. "Perfect."

"Okay," Grace said as she put her hands on the boys. "It's almost time Aunt Ella met her groom for their first look."

Grace and Ava went down the hall each holding Ella's hands, as the children followed from behind. "Stop," Shelby said. "Okay, go."

Ava laughed as she said, "She's so bossy."

Shelby pointed to the fireplace and said, "Ella, please stand directly in the center, Grace can you move the basket of kindling out of the way?"

Ava pursed her lips before telling the kids. "She's the best photographer in the world."

Maddie looked up at Ava and said, "Mommy said you are the best designer in the world and I'm just like you... a fashionista."

Ava kissed her on the top of her head. "I'm going to teach you so much."

Maddie clapped her hands and said, "Yay."

Then Shelby asked Grace and Ava to each stand to Ella's sides. When Mal and Hudson moved to look out the window, Shelby told them to stay right there as she snapped their photo. After taking another picture of the three women, she had the children stand in front of the women. "Everyone look at Aunt Ella. Great, now give me your biggest cheese smile."

"Aww," Grace said. "How cute."

"Okay, I'm going to see if the groom is ready to see his bride," Shelby said as she walked toward the hallway. "Wow, don't move." Shelby snapped his picture and then used her index finger to call Ella out to hall. "Very slowly," she told Ella.

Grace and Ava told the children not to move. "This is a very private and special moment for them."

Both Ava and Grace had tears in their eyes when they heard Ella tell Brody not to cry. Shelby captured the moment perfectly. Her camera must have been set to burst mode. She must have taken at least a hundred photos of Brody and Ella before his best man announced, it was time.

The ceremony was glowing with votives everywhere, seated in the front row was their immediate families and behind them their friends followed by rows of fireman from numerous companies. David winked at Ella as she walked past. Aunt Emily blew her a kiss. Jude mouthed the word, gorgeous. Their vows reflected their personalities and, their devotion to each other. "I give you this ring as a sign of my love."

Ella whispered, "Forever, right?"

Everyone laughed and when she kissed him, there wasn't a dry eye in the room.

The cocktail hour was equally romantic as everyone gathered in the Whittemore room. When Brody kissed Ella, everyone cheered. Maddie pointed to the large round chandelier and said she loved the big candles, Mal asked if he could show his brother the deer outside. "Look, there's a deer standing in the garden." Ava and Shelby stopped dancing, walked over to the window and smiled when they saw a buck, doe and three fawns. Shelby ran for her camera.

An hour later, the maître de said the ballroom was ready and it was time for the first dance. Everyone followed Ella and Brody into the ballroom. As everyone stood to the right of the dance floor, Brody held his hand out to Ella. Halfway into the song, "Broken Road" Ella and Brody stopped dancing and the quartet played, "We Are Family" as the children ran to the dance floor. Before the song was over, everyone was dancing.

As dinner was being served, each member in the bridal party offered their own toast to the happy couple. No one cried until Ava said, "I would like to thank God for blessing me with the most amazing best friends, I would not be standing here today if it wasn't for Grace and Ella. I owe them my life." Her raw emotion was felt by everyone. Both Grace and Ella had tears in their eyes listening and when she pointed to Ella and said, "You saved my life." Ella got up and hugged her. "I love you so much," Ava whispered in her ear. Then she leaned back and said, "I'm so happy for you."

Suddenly, every single fireman stood as Ella took her seat next to Brody. Then they placed one hand over their heart and pointed to Ava. With the other hand. Brody knew what they were doing. He stood up and said, "We are family. You are never alone."

Shelby reached up and took Ava by the hand and mouthed the words, "Thank you." to the fireman.

While the adults feasted on beef bourguignon and tantalizing pesto encrusted black pearl salmon, the children danced to the music. Of course, Shelby caught their every move.

David's cellphone buzzed in his pocket. He told Aunt Emily and Jude it was South County Hospital. "Excuse me for a minute," he said, got up and left the room.

"Hello, yes, this is David Wayne."

"Mr. Wayne, I'm sorry to bother you, but your business card is the only thing we found in his pocket. There's no other identification. By any chance can you—"

"I'm on my way," David said and thanked the woman for calling. Then he went back inside and told Aunt Emily and Jude he had to go. After explaining the call, Aunt Emily agreed to stay, but Jude insisted on traveling back to Point Judith with David.

"I'm coming with you. Do you think it's one of your workers?" she asked as she picked her purse up off the floor.

"I'm not sure who it is," he said and told Aunt Emily to say goodbye to Ella and Brody for him.

A minute later, someone was wheeling a cart filled with large cupcakes, fancy desserts from around the world and a three-tier wedding cake. No one cared about dessert, as soon as the DJ played, "Little Crew" (Firefighter's Wedding Song) performed by, Sam Macgregor and Madison Wolfe every single fireman was on the dance floor dancing around Ella. Tears filled her eyes as soon as Brody stepped in front of her, pointed his finger at her and sang aloud, "I'll spend the rest of my life with you and I know I'll still want more."

CAST OF CHARACTERS

David Wayne ~ Self-made billionaire

    Emily Marshall ~ David's aunt and celebrity chef

    Grace ~ Real Estate Agent

    Ella ~ Grace's best friend and boutique owner

    Ava ~ Grace's best friend and boutique owner

    Shelby ~ Photographer

    Geraldine Prescott ~ Investor

    Henry ~ David's gatehouse keeper

    Jimmy ~ Bartender

    Steve ~ Homeowner

    Bill McGhee ~ Captain of David's yacht The Bill Pay

    Cory James ~ First mate

    Red ~ Homeless man

    Dr. Danny Ferris ~ David's neighbor

    Brody ~ Fireman

    Jude ~ Writer

QUOTE

"Love is that feeling in which the happiness of another person is essential to your own."

ACKNOWLEDGMENTS

Thank you, Lord for blessing me with the words to write my stories. Because of You, I have the best book friends in the world. To my family, readers and book club members— my heart is overflowing with gratitude. Your loyalty means everything to me. Shout out to Gwen Ackley. Back in 2021, my literary agent told me about her church hosting a book festival. My first book had just come out and I was terrified, but I attended and now I am so glad I did. I met the most amazing people and best of all, I met— a true book friend, Gwen. At the last minute, I reached out to Gwen and asked her if she would read *Salty Brine Beach*. As busy as she is, she didn't hesitate to lend me her sharp eyes. Many blessing to Gwen for coming to my rescue... again.

I hope everyone enjoys reading *Salty Brine Beach* as much as I did writing it.

If you would like to join my book club on Facebook, here's the link:
Bit.ly/Judy-Prescott-Marshalls-Book-Club

To sign up for my newsletter email me your full name and your mailing address. So I can send you some awesome book swag.
Bit.ly/JPMMonthlyNewsletter

Now, you can buy all of my books directly from me at my new book store. All books are signed, include a bookmark and a little book swag.

Bit.ly/4h8WuhV

Thank you again for your support and friendship, Judy.

ALSO BY JUDY PRESCOTT MARSHALL

The Be Strong Enough Series

STILL CRAZY

THE INN IN RHODE ISLAND

THE COTTAGE AT THE INN IN RHODE ISLAND

Spin Off Series

SWEET BLESSINGS

SWEET BEGINNINGS

The Lighthouse Series

POINT JUDITH

www.ingramcontent.com/pod-product-compliance
Lightning Source LLC
Chambersburg PA
CBHW050353030726
47503CB00006B/1837